STAGE

★ Abbi ★
Blind Ambition

by Geena Dare

 ORCHARD BOOKS

To Jeff RVDB

ORCHARD BOOKS
96 Leonard Street, London EC2A 4RH
Orchard Books Australia
14 Mars Road, Lane Cove, NSW 2066
ISBN 1 86039 643 7
First published in Great Britain 1998
Paperback original
© Sharon.Siamon 1998
Printed in Great Britain

☆**CHAPTER ONE**☆

Blair

Abbi Reilly hurried down the school hall. She was trying to juggle an armful of books and read her timetable at the same time. Why could she never, ever remember what class was next? Or where the classrooms were in this big old brick building? Stage School was so confusing!

In her hurry, she tripped on a loose floor tile. All the books and papers exploded out of her arms and spread across the shiny tiled floor. Abbi scrabbled to pick them up, gripping the timetable in her teeth so it wouldn't get away from her.

"Help! This is not happening. I'm going to be seriously late for French," she muttered to herself.

Abbi's mane of gold-blonde hair swirled around her as she dived for her books. It framed a heart-shaped face, high cheekbones and wide-spaced blue eyes. Everything about Abbi sparkled with energy, but at this moment, she looked like a spinning top, out of control.

She'd been looking forward to her first week of Stage School so much – had worked so hard to get in. And now, she had to admit it, she hated everything about the William S. Holly School, or 'Hollywood' as it was often called.

She had thought Stage School would be a whole new world, where she would learn to act and sing and dance. Instead, the teachers were even more heartless and strict than in her old school. The timetable was so complicated that she hardly ever saw her friends, Jenna and Lauren, who had been in the same audition group with her that summer. And she always seemed to be late, and lost. Like now! This couldn't be the right hall – there was no one else here.

"Can I help?" A familiar voice made her look up with a start. A girl had appeared out of nowhere, and stood smiling down at her. She was smaller than Abbi, with short blonde hair and a lovely smile. It was a face Abbi knew well, a voice she'd heard every week on TV, from seven to eight on Tuesdays.

Abbi blushed scarlet. She took the timetable out of her mouth and managed to stammer. "You're...Blair...Blair Michaels!"

The girl nodded.

"You're my favourite TV star," Abbi gasped. "I watch every episode of *My Life*. I think you're the best person in the show!"

"Thank you." Blair tipped her head to one side. "I don't think I've seen you before. You must be a new student."

"You don't understand," Abbi said, still staring at Blair with a dazed expression. "I'm here because of you. You're the person who inspired me to become an actress…I knew you went to the school and that's why I auditioned! You look…so different in real life." Abbi knew she was talking too much, but she couldn't stop. This was really Blair Michaels, in the flesh, having a conversation with her!

Blair laughed, a lovely, tinkling sound. "That's what everyone says. I look different without make-up on."

"No, you're just so tiny and…and like a normal person. I want to be just like you!" she ended, blushing.

"You do?" Blair laughed again.

"I mean, I really want to act!" Abbi said. "That's why I came to this school."

"Well, you picked a good place," said Blair. "Are you on your way to class? Can I help?" She pointed to the fan of fallen papers. "It looks like you've had an accident."

"Oh…I…uh…I was trying to find out where I'm supposed to be next," Abbi murmured. Her bright blue eyes were riveted to Blair's face. She held up her timetable. "I never seem to be able to work out if it's Day One or Day Two, or which period it is."

Blair waved a graceful hand. "Oh, you'll get it all sorted out, don't worry," she said, as if school didn't matter in the slightest. "Did you hear they've put out the casting call for *Dracula*?"

Abbi scooped up all her notebooks together in one messy heap and stood up with a gasp. "You mean this autumn's show? They've called auditions, already?"

"The notice is up in the canteen," Blair nodded. She bent over and gathered up a few papers Abbi had missed. "Are you going to try out for a part?"

"Me?" Abbi gasped again. "Oh…I…yes!" She and her friends Lauren and Jenna had been talking about the school's production of *Dracula: The Musical* ever since the summer. They'd thought about little else except getting parts in the show.

"Good," Blair said. "What's your name?"

"Abbi…Abigail Reilly," Abbi stammered. She felt quite dizzy. Blair actually wanted to know her name!

"You have a wonderful look," Blair went on, "and I think you'd be perfect for the part of Lucy, the girl who gets bitten by Dracula. Be sure to try out for her and I'll put in a good word with Alan Steel."

Abbi's head was reeling. Blair called Mr Steel – the drama teacher and director of *Dracula* – Alan! Abbi had been crazy about Mr Steel from the moment she'd set eyes on him!

She stared at Blair. What must it be like to be her? A star with her own TV series, written about in magazines, appearing on talk shows, talking about teachers as if they were casual friends! It was everything Abbi wanted.

Blair gave a theatrical wave. "I've got to be going," she smiled at Abbi again. "See you at the auditions for *Dracula* then." And she breezed off down the empty hall.

Abbi sank to the floor again, leaning back against a wall of lockers. It was unbelievable! How could she go to French now, and sit at a desk muttering French verbs?

She forced her eyes to focus on the timetable still clutched in her hand. A glance at the clock told her it was eleven-thirty. It was first lunch period and Jenna and Lauren both had first lunch. They might be in the canteen right now.

Leaping to her feet, Abbi thundered down the corridor, her hair and book bag flying. Forget French! She had to find her friends and tell them all the news. *A wonderful look*, her heart sang. *Blair thinks I have a wonderful look!*

☆ CHAPTER TWO ☆

Forget French!

"Shouldn't you be in your French class?" Abbi's friend Jenna raised one eyebrow as Abbi stormed up to the canteen table, wild with excitement.

Jenna's black curly hair was braided in tiny strands, pulled high off her forehead and gathered in a clip. This accentuated her beautiful Caribbean features. Her tall, lean body was encased in a leotard and tights, over which she wore a floppy black sweater. Jenna was a dancer.

It was typical, Abbi thought, that Jenna would know her timetable better than she did. Jenna was always so organized!

Their friend Lauren sat at the end of the table. She was smaller than either Abbi or Jenna, and she had pale skin and blue-grey eyes. Her straight, silky fair hair was worn parted in the middle and tucked behind her ears. Right now, she was looking at Abbi with a puzzled frown. "You skipped French?" Lauren's voice was surprisingly strong and clear for such a small person. She had been taking singing lessons since she was six.

"Your French class was cancelled?" Jenna

suggested.

"Yes, no, wait!" Abbi paused to catch her breath. "I have so much to tell you!"

"The French teacher had a heart attack?" Lauren looked alarmed.

"I wish he would! No, I don't mean that, but Monsieur Le Blanc is such a pain. But it's nothing about French," Abbi panted. "Can't you just listen? There's a casting call for *Dracula: The Musical*!"

"Is that all?" Jenna relaxed her taut shoulders. "We know. Everybody's been talking about it."

"I can't go," Lauren sighed. "The first audition is the same night as my singing lesson. My parents say I have to keep up my classical lessons if I want to stay here."

"You're just going to have to miss your music lesson this once," Jenna said. "Auditions are more important!"

"But that's not all," Abbi plunged on. "I met Blair Michaels in the hall and–"

"Shh!! There she is," Lauren whispered. Blair had just strolled into the canteen and now every eye in the room followed her to her table. Abbi noticed that she chose a seat by the window. Probably wanted some time to herself. It must be hard when people were always gushing over you, Abbi thought.

"Everybody says she already has the lead part of Mina in the bag." Lauren was studying Blair.

"Well, she *is* a star," Abbi reminded her. "She's famous and beautiful and rich. I'd give anything to be like her!"

"She's not *that* good, and she sucks up to Mr Steel," Jenna muttered, turning away. "She walks around this school like she owns it."

"No!" Abbi burst out. "You're wrong, Jenna. She's great. That's what I wanted to tell you. I met her just now. She helped me when I dropped my books and she said I should audition for the part of Lucy." Abbi's eager face was glowing. "Isn't that unbelievable? She said she thought I'd be perfect...that's why I couldn't go to French...I thought I'd burst if I didn't tell you!"

Jenna tipped her head to one side and looked at Abbi. "Have you ever read the *Dracula* script?" she asked. "You're my friend and I think you're great, but I don't know if I'd say you were *perfect* for Lucy's part."

"I don't care what you think," Abbi said, her eyes wide. "Blair is a professional actress. She should know."

Jenna laughed. "You've got a bad case of hero worship, Abigail Reilly."

"Well, maybe!" Abbi cried. "But imagine acting in *Dracula* with Blair Michaels!"

Lauren's eyes were dreamy and far away. "I love the play *Dracula*. My favourite part is when the wolf comes crashing through the window...right into Lucy's bedroom!"

"Yes," Abbi shuddered, "and Lucy gets bitten by the vampire! If I play Lucy and Blair plays Mina, we'll be together on stage all the time. I could be on my way to being famous." Abbi did a little dance.

Jenna looked doubtful. "I still don't see how they're going to turn a horror story like *Dracula* into a musical. I think the drama department chose it just so they could have a showcase for Blair Michaels."

"Jenna! Where's your imagination?" Abbi grabbed Jenna's hand. "I can picture incredible dance numbers. How about Lucy, sleepwalking in the graveyard, or Mina's terrible dreams of swirling mist, and red eyes bending over her..." She pulled Jenna up and swung her round the canteen floor.

"Our music teacher says we can write the songs!" Lauren sighed. "Cross your fingers my parents let me stay at Holly." She held up both hands with her fingers crossed.

Abbi stared at her. "Are you still arguing with your parents about Stage School?" she asked.

"All the time." Lauren's lively face grew still and sad. "When we're not fighting they give me the silent treatment."

"You've got to make them see reason," Abbi said. "Stage School wouldn't be the same without you – we're a team!"

"Speaking of the team, here come the guys," Jenna announced.

Abbi grinned at the two boys working their way towards them through the crowded canteen. Matt and Dan had been in their audition group over the past summer. The five of them had sweated out three weeks of exhausting try-outs to win their places in the first year programme. They all knew the William S. Holly Stage School was a tough school, with an excellent reputation for training actors, singers and dancers.

As Matt approached the table a faint blush spread over Lauren's cheeks. There was something about the way his brown hair curled around his ears and the back of his neck, something about his smile and his walk, that made her feel weak at the knees. But she would die if Matt knew how she felt. It was enough just to be near him, even if he did treat her like his kid sister.

"I can tell by that smug look on your face you've heard about the casting call," Jenna told Matt. "You probably think you're going to be the lead dancer!" Jenna hoped Matt wouldn't even audition for a dancing part. He always made it so hard for her to concentrate – teasing her one moment and acting romantic the next.

"Me, I've always wanted to play Dracula," Dan said, putting on a fake accent from an old horror movie. "*I vant to drink your blood – aargh!*"

"If we were doing *Dracula* as a comedy, you'd be perfect," Matt laughed.

It was true, Abbi thought. No matter how hard Dan tried to be serious on stage, he always made people laugh. In real life he was funny and smart and knew a lot about the theatre. It was too bad Dan's ears stuck out and his mouth was too wide, and he was all elbows and knees!

Now Dan pulled his brown lunch bag out of his bag. So uncool! Abbi thought, but that was Dan. He never bought lunch like the rest of them, just ate peanut butter sandwiches, day after day.

He made one of his comic faces at Abbi. "Hey! You don't have first lunch. Aren't you supposed to be in French?"

"Oh, for heaven's sake. Forget the stupid French class!" Abbi cried. "I met Blair Michaels in the hall and I was so excited that she said I should try out for *Dracula* that I decided to skip French and come and tell you. But you're all acting like I've committed a major crime."

Dan shook his sandwich at Abbi. "Missing classes at William Holly *is* a major crime," he said. "Take it from someone who's been in trouble at school for most of his life. They don't fool around here. You have to keep up an average 'A' grade to be allowed in the school shows."

"I've just had the most exciting moment of my life,' Abbi moaned, "and all you guys can do is talk about how I'm missing a class. I've got plenty of time to get an 'A' in French. But right now, I have to get a part in *Dracula*. We all do."

"The casting call is for Thursday," Dan said. "That gives us two days to get ready." He pulled up the sleeves of his baggy old sweater.

"How?" Abbi tossed back her cloud of hair and her eyes sparkled as she looked around her group of friends. "How do we get ready?"

"Read the play," Dan shrugged. He held up his dog-eared copy of *Dracula*. "Sir Anthony Hopkins says he always reads his part a hundred and fifty times before he does a scene in a film."

"Then that's what we'll do," Abbi said. "I want the part of Lucy more than anything in the world!"

Ever since she had come to William S. Holly, Abbi had dreamed of a lead role, a starring part to sink her teeth into. It made her shiver to think that this could be it. How could she possibly wait till Thursday?

☆CHAPTER THREE☆

What an Entrance!

"So you think you're somehow above the rules of this school?" It was Thursday morning and Monsieur Le Blanc was standing over Abbi. He tapped one long skinny figure on his trouser leg and waited for her to answer.

To Abbi, who had just read *Dracula* one hundred and fifty times, the French teacher was a frightening figure. The name Le Blanc suited him. His face was a pasty white, his hands were long, and thin strands of grey hair were pasted across his scalp.

Abbi stared at Monsieur Le Blanc in fascination. Look at those dark circles under his eyes, she thought. He would be perfect for the part of Dracula. And the way he rolled his *r*-s was really spooky!

"Are you listening to me, Miss R-r-reilly?"

The rest of the class waited in anxious silence.

"Uh, yes, sir!" Abbi came back to reality with a start. "About the class I missed. I was feeling..."

"Don't try to tell me you were sick!" he roared. "You were seen in the canteen with your *fr-r*iends!"

"That's what I was going to say," Abbi gulped. "I was feeling so hungry, I couldn't wait for second lunch."

Monsieur Le Blanc turned away angrily and strode back to the front of the class. "You are wasting my valuable time," he said. "I am warning you. If you miss another class without a proper excuse you will be permanently excused from French. And I think you know what that means."

Abbi sat rigid in her seat, blazing with embarrassment. She knew all right. At William S. Holly you not only had to have 'A' averages to be in a show – you had to keep up 'B' averages just to stay in the school. But the academic subjects were so boring – frustrating French, musty mathematics – she just couldn't keep her mind on them. Facts seemed to slide out of her brain like melted butter.

But the play! She now knew every detail about *Dracula*, especially the part of Lucy. Abbi fixed her eyes on her French book, but what she saw was herself as Lucy – with long flowing gowns, and flowers wound in her hair – and Blair Michaels as Mina, her best friend…

"*Écouter!*"

Abbi looked up and saw Monsieur Le Blanc's eyes burning into her like laser beams. "I see you didn't even hear my question," he said nastily. "What is the past tense of the verb *écouter* – to listen?"

Abbi's heart beat fast. She had no idea.

"Perhaps you should see me after school to discuss your hea*r-r*-ing." Monsieur Le Blanc smiled nastily.

"No!" Abbi's heart sank. He couldn't possibly keep her in! He couldn't. Not tonight! Auditions started right after school this afternoon and she couldn't be late.

☆

The Stage School auditorium was in semi-darkness. Jenna, Lauren, Dan and Matt sat halfway down the rows of seats. Around them, other groups of students laughed and chattered. In front of them was the lighted arch of the empty stage where *Dracula* would come together in the next ten weeks.

The senior students and teachers sat in the front row. Blair Michael's blonde head could clearly be seen in the centre. She leaned over to say something to Mr Steel and they heard his deep laugh.

"Buddies!" Jenna said scornfully. "Did you see how Blair looked at us as she walked past? As if we were dirt on her shoes!" Jenna twisted in the deep plush of the auditorium seat to look back up the darkened aisle. "Where on earth is Abbi?"

"She's talked about Blair and this audition non-stop for two days," Lauren muttered. "You'd think she'd be on time."

Dan stood up and scanned the big auditorium. "If she's not here in five minutes I'll go and see if I can find her," he said. "If I know Abbi, she's in trouble somewhere."

"Doesn't anything *ordinary* ever happen to Abbi?" Jenna asked. "She just seems to go from one crisis to the next. If we danced like that, we'd always have bruised knees."

"Come on, Jenna. Not everyone can be as in control as you," Matt teased. "The perfect dancer, high on her toes, without a wobble." His brown eyes looked at her wickedly.

Jenna hated him at that moment. Matt always zoomed in on the things she cared about. So what if she loved the discipline and control of ballet? It was the nearest thing to perfection she'd ever found!

Just then, there was a thunderous crash backstage as a lighting stand hit the floor.

"It's so dark in here! Where is everybody? I can't see—"

"Uh-oh..." Dan groaned. "Abbi!"

The next moment, Abbi blundered on to the middle of the stage, her wild gold-blonde hair lit from above, her arms flung out, her face on fire. She shielded her eyes with her hands and blinked out at the surprised faces in the first row. "Oh, there you are...Blair...and Mr Steel! I thought you'd all be on stage. I'm sorry I'm late, I—"

Mr Steel sprang to his feet. "That's all right, we were just about to ask everyone to come up on stage." He grinned at Abbi and motioned the rest of them forward.

"Hi, Abbi, I'm glad you made it," Blair Michaels swept forward and grabbed her hand.

"What an entrance!" Matt laughed as they wormed their way out of their seats. "No chance they'll miss our Abbi."

"But she doesn't do these things on purpose," Lauren defended her friend, as they ran down the aisle towards the stage. "They just seem to happen to her."

Jenna narrowed her eyes. "I don't trust that Michaels girl," she said. "Why is she being so nice to Abbi? Something's going on here, I'm sure of it."

☆**CHAPTER FOUR**☆

Casting Call

The stage was soon crowded with students, all of them straining forward to hear Alan Steel's next words.

"Dancers, over here," he motioned to his right. The dancers moved gracefully to the left.

"Singers, over there." Lauren joined a group of singers on the other side.

"Actors, in the middle." Abbi glowed with pride as she and Dan stepped forward. They were really here. They were going to do a show. And Mr Steel was so gorgeous. She loved the way his hair fell over his forehead, the way he shrugged his shoulders...

"You are about to create a musical version of *Dracula* – a great classic," Mr Steel began. "I suppose all of you know the story?"

"Dracula is this old guy who snacks on other people's blood!" one actor suggested.

There was laughter from the group.

"He lives in a dark castle and comes out at night as a bat," added one of the dancers.

"He's hundreds of years old and he will live

forever, unless somebody drives a stake through his heart."

"Everyone he bites, turns into a vampire, too..." came a voice from the singing group. "And then they go on and bite other people, and so on."

Mr Steel held up his hand. "Good. You've got the idea. Bram Stoker wrote **Dracula** almost exactly one hundred years ago. Since then, each generation that comes along gives it a different spin. Now, it's your turn. I want lots of ideas from all of you. This is your production – not mine, or the dance teacher's or the music teacher's."

He turned to the dance teacher, a slim dark woman who didn't look much older than her students. "Miss Adaman, did you want to say a few words?"

Abbi didn't listen as Miss Adaman spoke to the dancers about their part in the production. She caught Blair's encouraging smile from across the stage and hugged herself with eager anticipation. She knew every single word of Lucy's speeches. She said them over and over in her mind now until Mr Steel announced it was time for the actors to audition.

He began to pair the girls off to read the parts of Mina and Lucy. Blair's name was called – Mr Steel paused. He looked at the group of students on stage for someone to read Lucy while Blair read Mina.

"How about Abbi?" Blair suggested. "I think she'd be brilliant as Lucy."

"Too big and blooming," Mr Steel smiled. "Abbi

would overpower your Mina, who's small and dainty but tough as a steel spring. In the end, it's Mina who defeats Dracula, not all the big strong men."

Abbi felt as though she'd been hit in the stomach. Too big! The words hung like a neon sign over her head, and nothing else Mr Steel said came through the cloud of despair that settled over her.

Mr Steel chose a thin, weedy-looking senior named Marcia to read with Blair, and they began to say their lines.

"Oh, Lucy, you look so pale and tired. What's the matter?"

Abbi wanted to die.

Several other girls read the parts of Mina but there was no one nearly as good as Blair. Mr Steel would be an idiot to choose anyone else!

Later, as they took a break, Blair came over to her. "I'm so sorry," she said in a dramatic whisper. "I really don't want Marcia to get Lucy's part. She's such a drag – it's like acting with a dead fish." She gave Abbi's hand a quick squeeze. "I'd love it if you were Lucy…I don't think you're too big!"

Abbi flushed a deep red. "Thank you," she whispered urgently. "And thanks for trying to help."

"What are friends for?" Blair smiled.

Abbi felt dizzy with pleasure. Blair wanted to be her friend! "I love the way you make friends so fast here," she said. "At my old school everyone thought I was *too dramatic*. Here I have all the kids from my audition group – Lauren and Dan and Jenna and Matt – and now *you*! It's amazing!"

"It's the theatre," Blair shrugged. "We're all in it together."

At that moment, Dan appeared beside them. "Come on!" he whispered to Abbi. "Let's audition for the parts of the maid and the gardener. There are a lot of second-year people trying out, but I bet we have a chance."

Abbi saw Blair look Dan up and down. She was suddenly aware of how Dan's old clothes and scraggly hair must look to someone like Blair. "The maid is just a bit part. Blair thinks I might still have a chance for Lucy," she whispered back.

"I heard all the big parts will go to the senior students," Dan said. He looked at Blair. "Isn't that the way it works?"

Blair tossed her hair back. "Not necessarily. If someone has exceptional talent..."

"Hush over there in the wings!" Mr Steel's voice had an edge. "I might as well tell you now that I don't tolerate any talking during rehearsals. It breaks the actors' concentration, and it breaks mine."

Abbi felt herself turning bright red again. Dan had got Blair into trouble for talking. "I'm sorry!" she managed to mouth, as Blair turned away.

"Did you want to audition for another part, Abbi?" Mr Steel asked.

Abbi glanced desperately at Blair. What should she do? What did Blair want her to do? If she lost the part of Lucy and didn't audition for anything else, she'd be back stage painting scenery!

"Uh, yes!" Abbi blurted. "I'd like to try out for the maid's part, if that's all right?" As she took her place centre stage, she saw Blair slip into the front row of seats without even a backward glance. What had she done?

She looked for Blair as she and Dan ran up the sloping aisle of the auditorium after try-outs. But Blair had gone.

Jenna, Matt and Lauren were waiting for them outside the theatre. Lauren was jumping around impatiently. "What happened?" she asked. "Hurry up and tell me – I've got to dash off to my singing lesson."

"Mr Steel wouldn't even let me read for Lucy's part," Abbi groaned. "And there are hundreds of people auditioning..."

"Bad luck!" Lauren patted her arm. "Sorry, I've got to go. See you later!" And she hurried off down the corridor.

"I think you'd make a great Irish maid," Dan said. "It's a long way from Dracula and Lucy, the parts we really wanted, but I guess we can't all be stars. Somebody told me first year students usually just help with costumes and make-up."

"Well, I won't!" Abbi blazed. "I came here to act, not put on make-up!" She stalked off towards the front doors of the school after Lauren.

Jenna, Matt and Dan exchanged glances as they followed Abbi and Lauren. "How did the dance try-outs go?" Dan asked.

"Amazing!" Jenna said. "The dancers are going to represent the forces of good and evil in the play."

"That's right," Matt grinned. "Personally, I see myself as a big, bad bat."

"More like a creepy, crawly spider," Jenna laughed. "It's going to be exciting. We're going to be working out a lot of the dances ourselves!"

"When do you two hear if you've got a part?" Matt asked as they caught up with Abbi.

"Call-backs are announced on Monday," Abbi said. "After we audition again, Mr Steel will announce the cast. Dan says we have no chance, except for bit parts," Abbi sighed. "But Blair said– "

"Blair is just stringing you along," Dan shook his head. "We'll be lucky if we get a call-back even for the parts of the maid and gardener. Don't get your hopes too high."

Abbi just shook her head. What did Dan know?

As they walked together down the steps of William S. Holly, a red sports car was pulling up outside the school. Blair came lightly down the stairs behind them, opened the door of the sleek little car and slipped into the passenger seat. She gave Abbi a warm smile and a wave, but her glance just flicked over the other four.

"OOOH! Did you feel that chill?" Jenna shivered. "I don't think the great Blair Michaels likes us much."

Abbi was still basking in the warmth of Blair's smile. Blair proved you could shoot for the top – and make it. She wasn't going to give up. She might still get the part of Lucy.

☆CHAPTER FIVE☆

Call-Backs

It was Monday at last, the day the call-backs would be posted up. For Abbi, sitting through class after class was torture. Did she imagine it, or did Monsieur Le Blanc's teeth look kind of long and pointed when he drilled French verbs?

What a relief it was to get to acting class, where they could relax, stretch out their legs, and let out their feelings.

"I'm going to fly into pieces, I'm so nervous," Abbi burst out to Dan. "This day seems a hundred years long!"

At that moment, Miss Madden, the head of the drama department, swept into the drama studio. She wore a loose, flowing green tunic, and had an unforgettable, booming voice.

"All right, on stage, flat on your backs. Give yourself room to breathe," she told them, spreading out her arms.

In fifteen seconds they were all flat on the stage floor of the small studio theatre. Miss Madden took them through a series of stretch and balance exercises that sent the French verbs and algebra facts flying from Abbi's tired brain.

"Now!" Miss Madden cried. "I want you to shut your eyes and create a picture of who you are. Stop! Don't apologize for being too short, or too tall, or too fat, or having a big nose." Next to her, Abbi could feel Dan twitch with laughter. Miss Madden had a very big nose.

Abbi could suddenly see herself stretched out on the stage, with her hair spread out around her face. She started to think, *I'm too big*, and then forced herself to stop. She heard her mother say, *too wild, too reckless, talks too loud*. She shut that voice down with a bang. It was hard, this exercise!

"I want you to stop picking holes in yourself," Miss Madden said. "Accept yourself. Love yourself! We will practise this exercise every class until I see you come into this room feeling good about yourselves. We must face our fears and doubts and use them in our performance. Now – pair off for improvs, please."

Dan grabbed Abbi's hand. "Let's do an improvisation as the maid and the gardener, in case we get a call-back today," he urged. "I'll be the honest, but ugly gardener, who is in love with the maid. You'll be the beautiful servant girl who dreams of finding Prince Charming..."

Abbi glanced quickly at Dan. He was trying to be funny, but underneath she knew he was really telling her how he felt. She wished she could take him seriously, but he was just...Dan. Funny nose, big ears – he could never be Prince Charming!

☆

The dance studio was a long bare room, with a wooden floor, a wall of mirrors, and a barre on the opposite wall for the dancers to practise.

Jenna stood at the barre now, watching her image in the mirror as she warmed up. After only a few weeks of Stage School, this room already felt like home. The daily ballet exercises, that were a chore for some students, felt as natural as breathing to Jenna. They were part of the discipline of becoming a great dancer. She could never get enough of dancing.

Matt was down near the piano at the end of the room, laughing and talking with a group of girls when he should have been warming up for rehearsal. It was the one thing Jenna could never forgive him for – the way he treated dancing as if it was just for laughs. It wouldn't be so annoying if Matt was a bad dancer, but he could have been really good if he took it seriously! Why did he try to get by on looks and charm, when he should be working on technique?

The other students were gathering along the barre. Jenna saw that she was almost the tallest in the class. If she grew much taller, she would be too tall to be a ballerina! At home, she measured herself on the kitchen door frame, and she had grown almost three centimetres over the summer. And she was only thirteen – with years of growing still ahead.

☆

Lauren sat quietly in the music studio, waiting for the others to arrive. The room had thickly padded walls for sound-proofing. Like the acting studio, it had a sloping floor, with tiers of carpeted benches running down to a small stage. But while the theatre studio was painted black and had no windows, light streamed into the music studio from a bank of windows near the ceiling.

Lauren had tears in her eyes and she looked up at the light, blinking them back. She had asked her dad to drive her to school early, just to get out of the house, but she couldn't forget the worried *Where did we go wrong?* look on his face.

Her father often had that look these days and so did her mother and her brother Robert. They tiptoed around her as if she had some fatal illness.

Ever since that summer day when she dropped the bombshell, Lauren's family had been in shock.

"You can't just *go* to Stage School, pumpkin," her father had laughed. "There are auditions to get in."

"I know," Lauren had told them. "I've *passed* the auditions. I am in. I only went at first to help my friend Martha, but then she didn't get in, and I did. I really want to give it a try."

There had been an awful silence.

"You're always saying you want me to sing opera," Lauren pressed on. "At Stage School I'll learn how to dance and act, and perform on a stage. It will be good training for me."

"But the music..." Lauren's mother broke in. "It's all those dreadful musicals."

"You can't seriously want to sing *that*!" Robert had said.

"You're taking private lessons from the best singing teacher in the city," her father had added. "You can get performance skills once your voice has developed." He'd said it as though the case was closed.

They had never expected Lauren to be so stubborn. She had dug her heels in and refused to budge. She had always been such a quiet girl, a good girl, a treasure! They couldn't understand why Stage School was so important to her.

It was more important than anything else to Lauren. At William S. Holly she had met Matt, and now, being close to him was all that mattered. Nothing else – not singing, not performing, not even her friends. Lauren knew she could never tell Abbi or Jenna how she felt.

☆

Important notices at the William S. Holly Stage School were always posted in the canteen.

"It's a wonder we don't all get indigestion," Abbi said. "We eat in a state of nervous terror." She piled lettuce on her plate at the canteen counter.

"Salad?" Blair came up beside her. "Are you dieting, Abbi?"

Abbi looked up with a puzzled frown. "No, of course not."

"Good," Blair smiled, and went off with her loaded tray.

"You wouldn't diet, would you Abbi?" Jenna asked. "You know how dangerous it is."

"Besides," Dan laughed. "Eating salad isn't going to get you down to Lucy size in one day."

"Oh, so that's it!" Jenna exclaimed. "You're dieting to get the part of Lucy in *Dracula*!"

"Listen, guys, I'm not dieting. I just like salad." Abbi shrugged. "It's something to nibble when I'm nervous, and it doesn't sit in my stomach like lead."

"That's what they all say," Jenna said, following her through the check out.

"All who?" Abbi stared at her.

Jenna looked straight into her eyes. "People with eating disorders always have excuses when they are obviously under-eating."

"Jenna, lighten up!" Abbi could feel herself blushing. She turned away and marched towards their table, her tray held high. Lauren, Matt and Dan exchanged worried looks.

"Did Blair put you up to this?" Jenna pursued Abbi. "She's a horrible influence on you."

"What are you talking about?"

"I've seen you – trying to walk like her, and toss your head back the way she does, and do that little wave with your hand."

"Stop this! It's none of your business!" Abbi cried, but Jenna didn't stop.

"It's one thing to get you all excited about hopeless expectations, but when you start dieting so you can copy some shallow television star..."

Abbi slammed down her tray. "You, you..." she stammered. "They're not hopeless expectations. What's wrong with trying to get to the top? And what's shallow about being a star of your own TV show? You're so pure and noble about your old dancing...you make me sick! And I'll eat whatever I want!"

Jenna's face looked as if it was carved from stone. "Fine. If you want to listen to Blair, go ahead."

"All right, I will." Abbi's blue eyes were sparkling angrily.

"Listen, you two!" Dan waved his arms. "Peace. Go to neutral corners. Calm down."

But Jenna grabbed her tray and bag and strode away.

"Now look what you've done." Matt's usually laughing face looked serious. "I know that look of Jenna's. I'm usually on the receiving end of that stony stare. She's really furious."

"She had no business telling me what to do!" Abbi stood with her face flaming, her hands on her hips. "Jenna can go and jump in the lake, for all I care!"

Over Abbi's shoulder, Dan saw Blair watching the whole scene from two tables away. There was a strange look in her eyes as she watched Jenna's angry figure striding away. It's almost as if she stage-managed the whole thing, Dan thought.

"You actors get so worked up over auditions..." Matt shook his head.

"That's easy for you to say," Abbi groaned. "If you dance or sing you don't have to worry about call-backs. You all get to be on stage."

"Jenna just doesn't want you to get ill, Abbi." Lauren had been quiet up to now, but she hated to see her friends fight. In some ways they were so

much alike – both strong and stubborn, both determined to succeed in their own way.

Abbi felt sick. How could Jenna say those awful
things about Blair? How could she begin to think
she was a bad influence?

Just then, Mr Steel walked briskly into the
canteen and pinned a sheet of paper to the notice
board. It was the call-back notice.

The fight was forgotten. There was a stampede
of bodies across the room.

☆CHAPTER SIX☆

Blair is Late

Abbi wriggled her way to the front. Her eyes flew to the bottom of the list. Her heart did flip-flops. She read the list three times before she found her name: Reilly, Abigail. And there was Dan's name, right above hers! Reeve, Dan.

"Reeve and Reilly," she turned a glowing face to Dan. "We made it to the call-backs."

Abbi threw both arms around Dan and hugged him.

At the back of the crowd, Jenna watched Abbi and Dan's joyful bear hug. Other actors were looking thrilled or crestfallen, depending on whether their names were on that list. Jenna felt detached from it all. The acting world can be so cruel, she thought.

Only one girl seemed cool. It was Marcia, the weird-looking senior who had tried out for Lucy. To Jenna's surprise, Marcia elbowed her way through the crowd towards her.

"You're a friend of that girl Abbi, aren't you?" she asked.

"I thought I was." Jenna's tone was serious. "She

seems to prefer Blair Michaels' company these days."

Marcia nodded, blinking her black-smudged eyes. "Blair's got her eye on Abbi," she said.

"What's Blair up to?" asked Jenna. Their friendship might be over, but she was still curious.

"Her usual tricks," Marcia said, "and I should know. I've been in the same class with Blair for two years. Every play we do, it's the same thing. She finds someone to be her favourite, someone who will make her look good and be at her beck and call. Then she drops them when the show is over. I was her favourite in the first show we were in together. Now she doesn't even want to act with me."

"So that's why she wanted Abbi to try out for Lucy's part." Jenna said.

"Just tell her to watch out." Marcia lowered her heavy eyelids. "She uses people for her own little games."

Jenna watched Marcia walk away. Was she just jealous, she wondered, or was she right about Blair?

☆

Hurrying to the call-backs at three-thirty, Abbi made a plan of action. She would get Blair to ask Mr Steel one more time to let her read for Lucy's part. She wanted it so badly – why shouldn't she have it?

By the time Abbi arrived, Mr Steel was pacing the stage. "Where is Blair Michaels?" he bellowed.

"Um, she'll be here. I just saw her at the pay

phone," Abbi said hurriedly.

Dan shot her a look. They had passed the pay phone, and Blair certainly hadn't been there.

Abbi shook her head slightly. She had to try and cover up for Blair.

Sure enough, she turned up a few minutes later, and gave Abbi a cheerful wave as she joined the others.

"Are you going to commit to this production or not, Blair?" Mr Steel demanded in front of the whole group. "You can't make a habit of being late for rehearsals, you realize."

Abbi thought Blair answered like a truly professional actress. "I had another appointment," she said coolly. "It ran late. I apologize."

"Are you going to have other appointments that will interfere with getting to rehearsals on time?" Mr Steel didn't waver. "Because if so, I think you should withdraw from the production now."

Abbi sucked in her breath. Blair not in the show? That would be a disaster!

"No, I'm sure I can make rehearsals," Blair said, still cool. "Let's get on with it, shall we?"

Abbi, Dan, and the other juniors watched as the senior students read for the lead parts. Abbi didn't dare ask Mr Steel to let her read for Lucy now – not after his angry outburst. Not when it seemed he was deliberately choosing people Blair didn't like to read for parts!

She saw Blair roll her eyes as Marcia read the Lucy part. Then a tall, clumsy boy read the part of Harker, Mina's boyfriend. Blair didn't look happy about him, either.

Finally, there was Dracula. What was Jake Lamont even doing in Stage School? Abbi wondered. He couldn't act, he stuttered horribly, and was so shy he could barely look any of the others in the eye. And he was supposed to be the fascinating, evil Count Dracula? Only if they were playing it for laughs.

Sure enough, at the break, Blair was fuming. "That stupid Alan Steel!" she hissed in the dim space behind the backstage curtain. "It's going to be bad enough having that gothic nightmare, Marcia, drooping around as Lucy. But if I have to put up with Jake..."

"It must be hard," Abbi said, "when you're used to working with a professional cast."

"Oh, don't get me wrong," Blair shook her head. "I love just being part of the school play like a normal person. I'm glad I have time between shooting episodes of *My Life*. I was really looking forward to this. Instead I've got Jake muttering 'I-I-I c-c-c-an't t-t-tell you w-w-what a p-p-pleasure–'" She stopped suddenly, flushing pink.

Abbi turned around. Jake had come quietly through the curtain while Blair was imitating his stutter. He looked really upset.

"Jake, that didn't come out the way I meant it..." Blair went over and looked into his face. "What can I say?"

"N-n-nothing!" Jake managed to stutter.

Abbi felt sorry for both of them.

"Abbi, Dan, did you two still want to audition

together for the maid and gardener's parts?" Mr Steel parted the curtain and strode backstage. "Where are you two?"

"Right here," Dan pulled Abbi on stage. "We added a bit to the scene, just to give you an idea of how we see the characters," he explained. "We can take it out if it doesn't work – I mean if you don't like it..."

"Look, I said I wanted your ideas. Don't apologize," Mr Steel said, as he walked to the front to watch. "Quiet!" he bellowed. "Abbi, set the scene for us."

Abbi stepped centre stage. "It's the second act," she said. "Lucy has just died from loss of blood. I'm her friend Mina's maid. The gardener is bringing me garlic wreaths to keep the vampire away." She mimed taking an armful of garlic from Dan, and spoke in the maid's accent.

"I don't think this old garlic is going to save Miss Mina. She's so weak, and those little puncture marks on her throat won't heal!"

Suddenly, Dan sprang to an imaginary window. "What's that?"

"It's that ugly big bat again. It keeps flapping its wings against the glass, as if it wanted to get in." Abbi's voice sank in terror.

"I'll keep watch from the garden, Miss," Dan said bravely. "I won't let anything get in that might harm you."

Mr Steel held up his hand. "Very good!" he said. "I'd like to have some other people read for the part before I decide."

Abbi and Dan went back to their seats and listened to the rest of the try-outs. When they were over, Mr Steel called them all to the stage once more.

"This is it," Abbi whispered. "He's going to announce the cast."

☆ CHAPTER SEVEN ☆

Warnings!

"Before I announce the cast," Mr Steel told them, "I've decided not to have understudies for the roles in *Dracula*. I'm counting on each of you to be here to play your part. You can't get sick, you can't drop out, and you can't–" here he glanced at Blair, "suddenly decide you have something more important to do."

There were nods of agreement.

Mr Steel looked at his list. "Then here's our cast for *Dancing with Dracula*." A lock of hair fell over his eyes and he pushed it back. Abbi held her breath. He looked so handsome, standing there, but couldn't he just hurry and get it over with!

"Mina will be played by Blair Michaels, her fiancé by Geordie. Marcia will play Lucy, and Jake Wentworth will be Count Dracula. Those are the four lead parts." Mr Steel paused.

Abbi swallowed hard. She could feel a large lump of disappointment choking her – she had wanted to be Lucy so badly! Dan squeezed her arm and Abbi could see he had his fingers crossed. There were still the minor parts.

"The part of Dr Von Helsing will be played by Mike," Mr Steel went on. "Abbi will be the maid, and Dan the gardener."

He went on to list the backstage crew, the stage manager and her assistant, the prompter, the costume designer, props, and make-up managers, the lighting and set design crew.

It was a long list, and Abbi had stopped listening when her name was called. The maid wasn't a main part, but at least she was in the production. And she and Dan could really make something of their parts, she was sure.

"There's one more thing," Mr Steel's voice broke through the happy haze in Abbi's brain. "You're all going to feel like a family before this is over. I know you've heard that before, but in the theatre it's true. You'll have lots of disagreements but I'm counting on you to support each other for the next eight weeks."

He gazed around at the silent group. "That's it. Go off and celebrate and I'll see you back here again tomorrow, at three, sharp!" He threw a last warning look at Blair.

Abbi noticed that Blair didn't stick around with the others for congratulations. She grabbed her coat and ran out of the auditorium doors. Abbi thought she looked upset.

"I can't believe Mr Steel is being so mean to Blair," Abbi said to Dan. "He's being so hard on her. She just wants to be one of the group, and he keeps picking on her."

"Can't you forget Blair for one minute?" Dan

said. "You, the beautiful and talented Abbi Reilly, got a part. You should be swinging from the ceiling. Let's go and celebrate!"

"I have to go home and babysit for my little brother," Abbi groaned. "But I've just got time for a coke in the canteen."

"I don't have any change..." Dan turned out his pockets.

"My treat!" Abbi laughed. Poor Dan, he never had any money.

☆

The entire cast of *Dracula: The Musical*, including the dancers and singers, was to meet at three the next afternoon.

Abbi and her friends gathered in the canteen for a quick bite to eat before their first rehearsal. Only Jenna was missing. Abbi could see her on the other side of the room, sitting with Marcia. Her heart gave a lurch. She was sorry she'd quarrelled with Jenna. If only there was some way to make it up – they had been so close.

But at that moment, Blair came weaving through the crowded canteen. She glanced quickly at Jenna and Marcia and then came over to Abbi's table.

"Here comes our star," Matt said under his breath as she approached.

Abbi forgot Jenna. Imagine, Blair, sitting at their table!

Matt pulled out a chair for her. "Welcome to the Table of the Totally Terrified," he grinned. "*Dracula* is our first show."

Blair gave him a dazzling smile. "You don't look like anything would frighten you," she said, sliding into the chair.

"Matt's a brilliant dancer," Abbi said. "And this is my friend Lauren Graham," she introduced Lauren. "She's in the music programme. You've met Dan, the gardener."

Blair nodded briefly at Lauren and Dan, then turned the force of her gaze back to Matt. "Where did you train, before you came to Stage School?" she asked him.

"Here and there," Matt shrugged. "Nowhere special. I just sort of pick things up, naturally."

"I'm sure you do..." Blair gave him another glittering smile.

Lauren felt icy cold. No wonder Blair liked Matt – he was one of the best-looking guys in the school. But she acted like the rest of them weren't even there!

Matt looked flattered, and confused. A silly grin began to spread over his face.

Lauren stood up suddenly, knocking over her bottle of mineral water. "I...have to go..." she stammered. "See you at rehearsal."

The spilled water flooded across the table. Blair flung herself back in her chair. She did it in such a way that Matt had to catch her. For a moment she leaned against him, looking up at him with her bewitching smile.

Lauren couldn't watch any more. She turned and fumbled through the crowded tables towards the door.

Matt laughed, and moved away from Blair. "I guess I'll catch up with Lauren," he said. "See you in the theatre."

Abbi reached for some napkins to stem the tide of water, and Dan picked up the bottle. The moment was over.

Blair was staring after Matt. "I'm sorry, did I miss something? Are Matt and that girl special friends?"

"No," Abbi hesitated. "It's not like that."

"Well, he certainly took off in a hurry," Blair said.

"He was just trying to act cool," Dan said. "He's not used to big stars throwing themselves into his arms."

"Dan!" Abbi cried.

Dan grinned, clowning again. "Hey! It's almost three," he said. "Do you still want to go over your French verbs before rehearsal, Abbi?"

"I don't think we have time," Abbi said. "I'm positive I'm going to fail! How could Monsieur Le Blanc give us a test the first week of rehearsals?" She slammed her can of grape juice down on the canteen table, her eyes flashing. "I wish I could give up French."

"Well, you can't," Dan shrugged. "And remember – you not only have to pass French, now that you're in *Dracula*, you have to get an 'A' to stay in the show."

"He's right," Blair nodded. "It's one thing they're really strict about here."

"But it's absolutely hopeless," Abbi moaned. "Half those verbs I've never heard of in English!"

"I'll help you after rehearsal," Dan promised.

☆

Rehearsal was magic for Abbi. "Blair is so wonderful," she whispered to Dan. "So cool and controlled, and did you see how she brings Mina to life!"

At the end of the rehearsal, Blair rushed up and handed Abbi a note, sealed in an envelope. "Can you give this to Matt?" she panted. "I've got to go and get my lift."

Abbi pictured the red sports car waiting at the bottom of the school steps. "Sure," she said. "I'll make sure he gets it."

As she and Dan left the theatre, she watched for Matt's dark head above the crowd in the packed hallway.

"I wonder what's in here?" she said, holding up the envelope.

"Blair said it was a note for Matt," Dan grinned.

"I know that. I mean, I wonder what Blair wrote?"

"You've got enough to worry about, without getting mixed up in this," Dan warned. "Remember – fifty irregular French verbs?"

"Ugh! Don't remind me." Abbi suddenly glimpsed Matt, talking to Jenna near the door. "There he is."

She dashed over to Matt, nodded coolly to Jenna and held out the note. "This is for you," she said, and turned away.

"Uh…thanks," Matt stared at the note.

He ripped open the envelope and pulled out a

single sheet of paper.

> *Dear Matt,*
> *I'm sorry if you thought I was too pushy today. I didn't realize Lauren Graham had already staked a claim. I didn't mean to embarrass you both. Please tell her that I won't bother you again.*
> *Let's be friends...*
> *Blair*

"What is it?" Jenna asked. Matt's face had turned from bright pink to pale. He looked awkward and embarrassed as he stared down the hall after Abbi.

"What did she say?" Jenna asked again.

"It's not from Abbi..." Matt mumbled. He crumpled the note and stuffed it in his pocket. "Sorry, Jenna, I've got to go."

☆

Abbi and Dan took the bus to her place after school. She lived in an apartment block in the centre of the city. She and her mother and younger brother, Joe, had moved there after her father had gone to Australia. Some day, Abbi's mother promised, they'd have a house of their own again.

Abbi wasn't holding her breath. They'd lived in Grandview Towers for four years. It was all right, especially since the summer when she and her Stage School friends had discovered the garden in the centre of the complex. All through auditions the garden had been their refuge from the world.

Abbi used her key to let herself and Dan into the courtyard.

"Dan, look!" Abbi gasped in dismay. An early frost had shrivelled the leaves on the roses and chilly autumn breezes swirled bits of paper around the concrete benches.

"We can't study here," Abbi shivered. "It looks so cold…and lonely, and deserted!"

"We could keep our coats on…" Dan suggested.

"I can't learn French verbs when I'm warm, let alone when I'm freezing!" Abbi closed the court-yard door with a bang. "You'll have to come up to my place."

"But won't your mother have a fit if she finds me there?" Dan protested as they ran for the stairs.

"We've got half an hour before she gets home," Abbi panted. "It's a stupid rule, anyway – no guys in the place! What does she think I am…a baby?"

Abbi made Dan a peanut butter and jam sandwich and sat down at the kitchen table with her legs twisted around the chair rungs, and the French book flat in front of her. Her brother Joe's computer game noises came through the closed door of the living room.

"I can't concentrate with all that BOOM, BOOM, KAPOW! stuff going on," Abbi groaned.

"Come on, Abbi. You learned Lucy's dialogue and the maid's part without even trying. What's so different about a few French verbs?"

"They just lie there – like squiggles on the page. When I look at them I see Monsieur Le Blanc's terrible face looking back at me. Did you ever notice how pointed his teeth are?"

"Abbi! You've got to try to keep your life

separate from the play." Dan shook his finger at her. "Your French teacher is not a vampire!"

"No, but my little brother is!" Abbi burst into laughter as her brother Joe burst through the door. He was dressed in a full Dracula costume – a long flowing black cape, red sash, and a set of plastic fangs. His spiky red hair stood up in points.

"I am the dread Count Dracula..." he lisped through his teeth.

"You're going to get it if Mum sees you in her evening cape," Abbi giggled.

Joe whipped the fangs out of his mouth. "Hi, Dan," he said. "I think it's so cool that you're going to be in a Dracula play. Do you get to bite my sister?" He put the fangs back in and swirled around the room, holding the cape in front of his face.

"He's better than Jake," Abbi laughed.

They were having such a good time with Joe, they didn't hear the door opening behind them

Abbi's mum, trim in her dark business suit, stood staring at them.

"Abbi! What is Dan doing here?" her mother demanded.

☆CHAPTER EIGHT☆

Wicked Surprises

"I think I'd better go," Dan said, jumping up.

"Mum, wait! I need to talk to you," Abbi begged. But Mrs Reilly had just spotted Joe. "What are you doing in my evening cape...AND MY BEST RED SILK SCARF?" her voice rose to a shriek. "What's going on here?" Abbi's mum tried to unpin her satin evening cape from Joe's shoulders while she glared at Abbi.

"Today was the *Dracula* rehearsal. I've got a part!" Abbi rushed ahead, trying to explain. "Dan is helping me with my French so I can stay in the play."

Abbi's mum's face changed. She held out her arms. "Abbi, that's wonderful! Congratulations! How about you, Dan? Are you in the show, too?"

"I'm the humble gardener." Dan made a comic bow and paused with his hand on the doorknob.

Mrs Reilly collapsed at the kitchen table with a sigh. She brushed back her short brown hair with a tired gesture. "All right. Let's talk."

"I'm thirteen," Abbi began. "If I'm old enough to look after Joe, why can't you trust me?"

"I do trust you," Mrs Reilly said. "That's not the point. The rule is – no boys inside when I'm not at home."

"Dan's not a boy!" Abbi cried. "He's Dan."

Dan flushed and looked down at the table.

"He's nice," Joe added. "I wish he was my baby-sitter, instead of my screaming sister!"

This was going in the wrong direction, Abbi thought. She put the kettle on for a cup of tea for her mother while she planned what to say next.

"My friends help me with Joe," she told her mother. "He'll do anything for Dan, or Matt."

"I'm sorry," Abbi's mum shook her head. "I know Joe is a handful sometimes, but a rule is a rule."

Abbi felt like exploding. "You don't trust me at all, do you?" she shouted. "And if Dan doesn't help me, I'm going to fail my French!"

"I think I'd better go," Dan muttered. "I'll meet you in the canteen tomorrow morning."

After Dan had gone, Abbi ran to her room and slammed the door. Sometimes she really missed her father. She could always reason with him! She yanked a piece of paper out of her notebook and started a letter to him, telling him all about the show. The page of French verbs lay untouched on her desk.

☆

Lauren sat in the noisy canteen the next morning, pretending to study her music. Actually, she was waiting for one glimpse of Matt. The *Dracula: The Musical* tunes were easy compared with the usual stuff she sang, so she barely needed to glance at them. She just had to see Matt, before her day began.

They always met up at their table before classes, but this morning Abbi was studying French with Dan, and Jenna was sitting with Marcia.

To her surprise, Lauren suddenly saw Matt crossing the room towards her, not with his usual light-hearted swagger, but as if he had the weight of the world on his shoulders.

"Hi." He barely looked at her. His beautiful brown eyes were fixed on the floor. "I need to talk to you, Lauren."

It was as if they were suddenly strangers.

"What's the matter?" Lauren looked up quickly into his face. The teasing, laughing smile was gone. Matt looked nervous, and watchful.

He sat down opposite her and clenched his hands together in front of him. He glanced around quickly to make sure no one was listening.

"I didn't know…how you felt, Lauren," he stammered. "I'm sorry if I ever…I think of you as a friend."

Lauren felt her whole body flush with embarrassment. She thought she was going to be sick.

"Who told you?" she managed to say.

"Abbi…gave me a note," Matt was obviously feeling so awkward he could hardly speak, either.

Abbi! Lauren's embarrassment switched to anger – a burning fury that she had never felt before. Her tongue felt paralysed, so she could only shake her head. No, no, no! This couldn't be happening!

"I hope we can still be friends," Matt struggled on, his face screwed up in concentration. "I would never want to hurt you."

Lauren's whole world was crumbling. She had to say something. "It must be a joke," she managed to croak. "Someone's been playing a trick on us..."

"You mean you don't–"

Lauren shook her head and tried to laugh. "Of course not. We're all just friends. The whole thing is ridiculous."

The clouds cleared from Matt's face and he beamed his old smile at Lauren. "Whew! What a relief. You don't know how I've been worrying." He bounced to his feet with the old Matt confidence.

"Abbi told you that?" Lauren managed to ask. She could hardly believe Abbi would betray her like this.

Matt nodded. "She brought me a note from the great Blair Michaels...Well, I've got to get to dance class. See you first lunch?"

"Sure." Lauren tried to smile a normal goodbye as Matt hopped across her outstretched legs. He passed Abbi and Dan on their way in.

Dan was still rattling off verbs, and Abbi was repeating them in French. They stopped when they saw Lauren, standing with her music clutched to her chest.

"How could you, Abigail Reilly?" Lauren hissed between clenched teeth. "Jenna was right. You're a different person now you're hanging around with Blair."

Abbi's jaw dropped in astonishment.

"Lauren – wait! What's wrong? What happened?"

"Don't play innocent," Lauren was shaking with fury. "That note you gave Matt, telling him how I felt about him! I never want to speak to you again."

"It wasn't my note, it was Blair's," Abbi gasped.

"You must have told Blair...how else would she know!"

"Lauren, everybody knows how you feel–"

"Matt didn't..." Lauren twisted away from Abbi's hand on her arm, "...not until he read that note. He came in here...you've ruined everything!"

"Oh, Lauren, I'm sorry! But I didn't even know what was in the note, did I, Dan?" Abbi appealed to Dan. "You were there."

Dan threw up his hands. "I'm staying out of this!"

Lauren turned to walk away.

"Wait a second," Abbi grabbed her shoulder. "I can't believe you think I'd write Matt a note like that. I'm your friend!"

"I thought you were!" Lauren turned back to her, her face pale and furious. "But not any more. Stay away from me, and stop spreading stories – you and your precious Blair Michaels!"

"This is awful!" Abbi moaned, as Lauren marched off. "Lauren must think I gossiped to Blair about her and Matt. But I didn't. Blair must have guessed."

At that moment the bell for first class rang, and the canteen emptied like water sucked down a drain.

"My French test!" Abbi suddenly remembered.

"You'll be all right." Dan gave her a thumbs up signal as they raced for the door. "I'll see you later – at rehearsal!"

☆

"How was the test?" Dan asked on the way into the theatre.

"Terrible!" Abbi groaned. "I kept thinking about my fight with Lauren. I'm going to plead with old Le Blanc to let me do it again. Do you think he will?"

"Pleading never worked for me." Dan smiled. "But then, I don't have your face."

At this second rehearsal Mr Steel really got down to business, blocking each move on stage in the first act.

All Abbi's worries flew out of her head as they walked through the play. She had always imagined actors moved freely around the stage, the way they did in improvisations. But Mr Steel planned every move. He used chalk marks on the floor to show the actors where to stand, how far to walk, where to turn. Every time they sat down or stood up, they jotted a note on their scripts.

"It's like learning a dance!" Abbi whispered to Dan. She picked up the moves quickly.

"That's excellent," Mr Steel congratulated her. "You're going to be a good actress some day, Abbi."

Abbi turned, pleased, and saw Blair watching. Back stage, at the break, she pulled Abbi aside.

"Did you give your gorgeous friend Matt my

note?" she asked her. Abbi nodded. Suddenly she remembered Lauren, and how miserable Blair's note had made her. "Lauren is furious that you told Matt she liked him," she said.

"Is she?" Blair sounded astonished. "I thought everybody knew but me."

"Well, Lauren didn't think so," Abbi said. "I guess I've lost a friend now."

"I don't know how she could think Matt wouln't guess. She sat there making cow eyes at him all the time," Blair shrugged. "It was so obvious."

"Matt never noticed," Abbi sighed. "He's too wrapped up in himself."

Blair smiled. "I'm sorry Lauren is mad at you, when it was really my fault, but maybe I can make it up to you. I have some amazing news!"

She pulled Abbi to the side of the stage where they could talk without being overheard. "This is top secret. There might be an opening in the cast of *My Life*. One of the actors is moving on to another series – she's really getting too old for our show and they want a new, younger actress."

Abbi felt the skin on her arms prickle. "Which part is it?" she asked. She knew the characters on *My Life* inside out.

"I can't tell you that until we're sure she's leaving," Blair shook her head. "But you'd be perfect for the part. I'm going to see if I can get you an audition."

Abbi felt a surge of excitement. "You'd really do that? You mean I could be on TV?"

"Of course," Blair smiled. "You're my friend.

Can you get me a photo of yourself to show them?"

"We had to get head shots taken for auditions last summer – I could give you one of those."

"Perfect," Blair said.

☆CHAPTER NINE☆

Getting in Deeper

Over the next three weeks of rehearsal, Abbi hugged Blair's promise to herself like a warm pillow. She had given Blair her photo, now she had to wait for a chance to audition for *My Life* – a real TV show!

Just thinking about being on TV got her through her French and mathematics. It helped make Jenna's cold glances and Lauren's sad face bearable when she passed them in the hall.

Abbi still missed them terribly. She missed their long phone conversations in the evening, and getting together in the canteen. Maybe, once she had a part in *My Life*, they would understand how she had to give up everything – just for a while.

"Have you heard when the audition might be?" Abbi's blue eyes were intense as she leaned across the canteen table. She and Blair were alone, but someone at one of the other tables might be listening

Blair shook her head. "We're still not sure if… the other girl has to leave. The poor kid. She looks older every day. They keep having to get her new costumes."

"Jenna worries about getting too tall, too," Abbi said, looking across the room to where Jenna was standing by a window, talking to Lauren.

"Do you still talk to her?" Blair asked.

Abbi shook her head. She hadn't spoken to either Jenna or Lauren for weeks. Seeing the two of them together gave Abbi an odd feeling in the pit of her stomach. She turned her attention back to Blair. "How about me?" she asked. "Mr Steel said I was too big to play Lucy. Do you think I'd be too big for TV?"

"Oh no! Don't worry." Blair's tinkling laughter reassured her. "If this part comes up you'll be perfect for it."

Abbi sighed happily. Just imagine how it would be to act for real, to have people picking out new clothes for you to wear in each episode; doing your hair and make-up so you always looked fantastic – just like Blair!

☆

"Everybody on stage, please, to run through Act Two," Mr Steel boomed from the back of the auditorium the next day. "Quickly, now. We're falling behind our schedule."

Abbi hurried to her position centre stage. It was already the end of September. Only two short weeks from now *Dracula* had to be ready to be performed in front of an audience.

"All right, let's roll!" Mr Steel called. "Remember, PROJECT YOUR VOICES! I want to hear you clearly in the back row!

Abbi felt as though her brain was a pot of

boiling pasta. There were so many things to remember – where to stand, which way to move, what to bring on stage, what to take off. And now, projecting her voice to the back row.

She had no idea acting could be so complicated.

She and Dan ran through their first scene as the maid and gardener. Now it was time for Blair Michaels, as Mina, to make her entrance.

"Ssh! Here comes my mistress," Abbi said in a loud stage whisper.

But Blair didn't appear.

Maybe she hadn't given Blair her cue loud enough. "Ssh! Here comes my MISTRESS!" Abbi roared again.

Still no Blair.

"Where is Miss Michaels?" Mr Steel came striding down the aisle, his hair dishevelled.

The stage manager, Terri, stuck her head through the back curtain. "She called a few minutes ago," Terri said. "She's stuck at the airport."

Stuck at the airport, Abbi thought. Blair's life is nothing like ours. She lives like a real star.

"Well, we're stuck until she gets here," Mr Steel threw down his script in disgust. "She's in almost every scene in the second act."

"Excuse me, Mr Steel?" Abbi said hesitantly. "Could I stand in for Blair? I think I know most of her blocking."

Mr Steel gave Abbi a long look. She was sure he was going to say no. Instead, he grinned. "Sure, let's give it a try. We *are* running out of time."

They started the run through. Abbi loved Act Two. Mina had some great scenes. Abbi's favourite part was near the end, when Dracula swept Mina into his arms for a final bite. They were going to use stage blood so that it seemed to be dripping down Blair's throat.

The trouble was, Jake couldn't even read his lines, let alone act like a vampire. He stood shyly in his jeans and green sweater and stuttered painfully. "C-c-come to m-m-me..."

It was hard to stay in character when Jake was so bad. No wonder Blair complained! Abbi thought. He goes all white and staring, and his arms are as stiff as boards. Still, they managed to get through the act without stopping.

"You were great," Dan panted as they ran off stage after their final scene. "But we're going to have a tough time if Blair keeps missing rehearsals. You can't be Mina and the maid, too."

"She's only missed a couple," Abbi defended her idol. "And I'm sure she doesn't need to rehearse as much as the rest of us. For professional shows, they only have a few weeks."

"That was a good run through, thanks to Abbi," Mr Steel told the cast. "But we have lost time with various problems, and Blair's constant lateness. We have to make it up if we're going to be ready for opening night. Please tell your families that you won't be home from rehearsal until six or seven, and we'll have to schedule dress and technical rehearsals for the next two weekends."

"Oh boy!" Abbi exclaimed. "I'm not looking

forward to telling my mum. What are we going to do about baby-sitting for Joe?"

☆

"Miss R-r-reilly, I am calling your mother." Monsieur Le Blanc glared at Abbi and shook a long, bony finger at her. "You did badly on the test and your term's work is atrocious!"

"Monsieur Le Blanc, you can't do that!" Abbi gasped. In the build up to opening night she had forgotten all about French. Now it was back, like Dracula's evil fog, surrounding her.

"The show is only two weeks away," Abbi choked. "My mother will have a fit. The school won't let me perform! Oh please, Monsieur Le Blanc, give me another chance!" Her words tumbled over each other.

"Hah! It is not my doing," Monsieur Le Blanc held up Abbi's French notebook and riffled through the pages. "Where are your homework assignments, eh? Where are your dictation errors written twenty-five times each? Where are your French poems and compositions, tell me that?"

Abbi nodded miserably. Her notebook was full of blank pages. What was Mr Steel going to say? She would let the show down. "If I make it all up by the end of the week," she begged, "if I hand in my notebook on Monday, will you reconsider?"

"This whole notebook, full? It is not possible!" Monsieur Le Blanc shook his head. "But I am a fair man. I will give you one more chance–"

"Thank you, Monsieur," Abbi seized his cold hand and shook it. "You won't regret it, I promise."

She grabbed her notebook and ran from the room.

☆

"I'm totally dead meat," Abbi groaned, showing Dan her empty book. "We have three-and-a-half-hour rehearsals all week, and on the weekend. I'll never catch up."

"Abbi, Abbi, Abbi – you're hopeless," Dan put his head down on his arms.

"Abbi is not hopeless," Blair said breezily, coming up to their table. "She's the best. Thank you for filling in for me yesterday. I had to go to New York, and then the plane couldn't land, and–" She stopped suddenly and looked at Dan. "What are you two looking so down about, anyway?"

"We have to rescue Abbi from total disaster," Dan said. "If this French notebook isn't handed in by Monday, she's out of the show."

"Blair doesn't care about things like that!" Abbi protested. "She's got her career to think about."

"Of course I care," Blair said. "Why don't you get Matt to help." Matt sat at a nearby table, chatting to Jenna and Lauren. Since Abbi's battles with her friends, he had gone back and forth between the groups, staying on good terms with everyone.

"I don't know..." Abbi said. "I can't picture Matt tutoring."

"I'll go and ask him," Blair volunteered, and sauntered towards the other table.

Dan and Abbi watched while Blair tapped Matt on the arm, and then stood looking up at his face in a pose of eager appeal.

☆62☆

"Isn't she great," sighed Abbi. "A real friend."

"She's a good actress, that's for sure," Dan muttered. "Look at her moving in on Matt."

Suddenly, Blair turned and marched back towards them. Her face was red as if she'd been slapped by a stinging blow.

"Uh-oh!" Dan said. "Trouble!"

"What did Matt say?" Abbi asked. "Will he help?"

"I don't want to hurt your feelings, so I won't tell you what he said." Blair's face was still bright pink. "Just take it from me, he isn't interested."

Later, Dan met Jenna in the hall. "What did Matt say to the great star?" he asked. "She looked annoyed."

"He said he'd help if Abbi asked him," Jenna reported, "but he wasn't doing it for Blair."

Dan grinned. "I don't think Blair is used to being turned down. No wonder her face was red!"

☆

At home, Abbi confronted a red-faced mother, as well. "Why didn't you tell me about these late rehearsals sooner?" she shouted. "How am I going to get a sitter for Joe at such short notice!"

"I didn't know," Abbi groaned. "Mr Steel just told us yesterday, and–"

"This Stage School!" Mrs Reilly began, and then bit her lip. "All right. I'll try to get Mrs Thomas to come in, but you know how Joe hates her looking after him."

Abbi took a deep breath and snatched her French notebook out of her bag. Now, if Mrs Thomas came, if she could make up her term work, and if Mum didn't get a phone call from Monsieur Le Blanc...

"I have to work," she announced. "No dinner for me."

"Abbi – you have to eat."

"I will, I will," Abbi promised. "But I write better when I'm hungry." She had been trying to cut down on food before her television audition. The TV camera added pounds, everybody said. Blair said if you put off eating, your stomach would shrink. It seemed to be working.

☆ CHAPTER TEN ☆

Disaster!

Monday morning, pale but triumphant, Abbi arrived in the canteen, flourishing a full notebook under the noses of Dan and Blair.

"My hand is falling off, but I filled the whole book." Abbi rubbed her sore wrist.

Dan flipped through her book. "Look at all this stuff you wrote! It's amazing!"

"And everyone says you were brilliant, filling in for me," Blair added. "Mr Steel seems to think you're his next big star..." She paused. "I'm going up to the third floor, if you want me to hand in your notebook."

"That's OK, I want to hand it to him personally," Abbi said, "before I lose it or spill something on it." She shoved the notebook in her bag. "This should stop old Le Blanc calling my mother!"

Abbi left the canteen and hurried up to the third floor to the French room. Monsieur Le Blanc was not there, so she carefully placed the notebook in the centre of his desk, where he would be sure to find it.

☆

Abbi went early to rehearsal. Today was very important – it was the day the actors finally put down their scripts. Abbi knew all her lines. In fact she knew almost everybody else's lines, too. The play had been running through her tired brain for days.

She tiptoed up the backstage stairs where she had made her embarrassing entrance four weeks before. What a change since then! Instead of a bare stage, she was entering Dracula's castle!

There were no lights on, but by now Abbi knew her way around the set. She was careful not to trip on the triangles of lumber that held up the flats, or Dracula's spooky black coffin.

Abbi peered into the coffin on her way past and her heart almost stopped! A figure, draped in a black cloak, lay in the coffin, its white face framed by dark hair,

Abbi leaped back with a scream. The figure slowly sat up.

"Jake!" Abbi shrieked. "What are you doing?"

"Trying to c-concentrate," Jake stammered. "G-getting into the r-role."

"Whew!" Abbi collapsed on to the stage floor. "You looked so real in there."

Jake climbed out of the coffin. He was wearing the Dracula costume. "It's a b-b-big day," he said. "B-b-ooks down!"

Abbi nodded. Her heart was still pounding from the shock of seeing him looking like a corpse. "I know. That's why I came early, too." But lying in a coffin concentrating wasn't going to help Jake sound like Dracula, she thought. She wondered if people would laugh when he stuttered. That would ruin the play!

The backstage door creaked open and someone else came up the steps. It was Maeve, the prompter. "Hi," she said. "You guys nervous about today?" Maeve had short brown hair, a shy smile and clear voice.

"Not with you on the job," Abbi grinned. "You're our lifeline from here on."

Maeve sighed. "At last I get to do something." The prompter hadn't had any work until now, when the actors would be saying their lines without a script. "I love what you do with the maid's part," she told Abbi. "I hope I get to be on stage next time."

"I'm sure you will." Abbi tried to imagine how she would feel if she had been chosen as the prompter, instead of having even a small role. She suddenly felt very lucky.

☆

Once all the actors were in position, Mr Steel held his hand up for silence. It was their first run through without scripts.

Jake, as Dracula, was just about to knock on the door.

Abbi, as the maid, answered.

"Good afternoon," Jake spoke in a deep, rich Transylvanian accent without a trace of a stutter. "Is the master at home?"

Abbi was so astonished at Jake's new voice, she forgot to curtsy. Wrapped in his black cape, Jake seemed to tower over her. She stared at him, speechless.

"Come in, sir," Maeve whispered from the prompter's box.

Abbi suddenly realized she must keep going – Jake was totally into his part and if she fumbled, he might lose it.

"Come in, sir," she curtsied, and reached for his walking stick. "The master and Miss Mina are in the garden. I'll tell them you're here."

She hurried off. Backstage, the other actors were whispering to each other.

"He's good!" Marcia whispered.

"What presence!" Dan said.

"Keep the scene going," Abbi urged. "Don't let him lose it."

They listened and watched from the wings as the play moved on. Everyone seemed to come alive with Jake's new performance. Blair was marvellous, Geordie struggled with his lines, but Maeve was there to help him.

Suddenly, *Dracula* seemed like a real play.

Mr Steel called a break.

"Should we say something to Jake?" Marcia asked. "About how well he did?"

"It's no big deal," Blair shrugged. "He's finally acting, that's all."

"I think Blair's right," Abbi nodded. "We might embarrass him."

"What a surprise," Marcia said nastily. "Abbi agrees with Blair. You'd think they were cloned, or something."

The music room in Lauren's house looked out on to the back garden. There were cedar trees and rambling roses. It was Lauren's favourite view, but the garden looked sad at this time of year.

She sat in the window seat, looking out and thinking about her role in the play. She was just part of the chorus, but she played a child who had been lured out into a wild part of the park by a 'beautiful lady in white'. The lady was Lucy. Dracula had turned her into a vampire, and when she called to the children, they could not resist.

Lauren shivered. I know that feeling. You feel drawn to something against your will. The longing is so strong you can't help yourself, even though it might be dangerous.

She moved restlessly to the piano stool. She had always lived such a safe life, in this big house, with her nice family. It was no use wishing she could go back. She was a different person inside, even though she still looked like the Lauren they knew.

The words to a song began to form in her head:

> *You think you can hold me*
> *But I have to go*
> *Out there, where nothing is sure*
> *Something is calling.*

Lauren reached for a scrap of paper and jotted the words down. Tears dripped on to the piano keys as she sang them softly to a melody that seemed to come from somewhere deep inside her.

"Lauren! It's nice to hear you singing again," her

mother stuck her head round the door. "That's a lovely tune. Is it something you're working on with Miss Bainbridge?

Lauren quickly tucked the piece of paper in her pocket. "No," she said, not looking at her mother. "I was just fooling around."

Tomorrow she would sing it at rehearsal – if she had the courage.

☆

The next afternoon, Abbi tore up the stairs three at a time. "Excuse me, Monsieur Le Blanc," she panted, "I wondered if you'd marked my notebook yet."

"Your notebook?" Monsieur Le Blanc gave her a cold glance. "I haven't seen your notebook. Are you telling me you handed it in, Miss R-r-reilly?"

Abbi felt her heart fall through the soles of her shoes. "I put it right there on your desk," she stammered. "Yesterday."

The French teacher looked down his long nose. "Is this some pitiful attempt to keep me from giving you a bad grade?" he demanded. "I warn you that in thirty years of teaching I have seen every tr-rick in the book!"

"It's not a trick!" Abbi choked back her anger. "I worked so hard – the notebook was completely full. Look, I have the dent in my writing finger to prove it!" She marched over to the desk and showed him.

"Please, none of your dr-ramatics," Monsieur Le Blanc waved her away. "I have no notebook here to mark. I have no choice but to give you zero."

"Please!" Abbi begged him. "My friends saw my book. They'll tell you."

"I'm sure your *fr-r*iends will say anything." Monsieur Le Blanc glared at Abbi, then stopped. "This is useless. I'll give you until tomorrow to produce this ma*r-r*vellous work."

"Thank you," Abbi managed to choke. Then she fled back down the three flights of stairs to the theatre. She just had to find Dan and Blair.

"What's the matter?" Blair asked, as Abbi burst through the backstage curtains. "You look ready to strangle someone."

"Who took my notebook?" Abbi shouted. "Monsieur Le Blanc says he's never seen it."

To her surprise, Blair turned away. "I have to see about my costume," she mumbled, and slipped off into the backstage shadows.

Abbi followed her, clattering down the stairs to the wardrobe room. Rows of costumes hung in black plastic bags.

"Blair!" cried Abbi. "Do you know something about my French notebook? You're not playing some kind of joke, are you?"

Blair's face was very pale. "Abbi, how could you even think that?"

"Well, you offered to deliver it to Monsieur Le Blanc for me..."

"But I didn't take it," Blair said. "Look, Abbi, you'll never know how much it means to me to have a friend like you – someone I can really count on. When you're famous, people crowd around you – sometimes it feels like they're sucking the life out of you – but none of them are your real friends!"

Abbi looked at Blair and for a moment she saw someone very different from the self-confident TV star. Blair looked lost, and alone. Almost like Mina when the vampire closed in on her near the end of the play.

"I'm sorry," Abbi gave Blair a quick hug. "I'm sorry I even suggested you took my notebook."

"But you were right," Blair said. "I do know something about it."

"Tell me!" Abbi insisted.

"You're not going to want to hear this." Blair's eyes were brimming with sympathy. "After you left the canteen…I overheard Matt telling Jenna and Lauren it might be a good joke if your precious notebook did get lost," Blair began.

"Matt–?" Abbi began.

"And then Jenna said she thought you needed to be taught a lesson, because you were acting like you were better than everyone else."

"I don't think that!" Abbi protested,

Blair put her hand on Abbi's shoulder. "Of course not. Your friends are just jealous because you have so much talent. The same thing happens to me, all the time."

"But, Matt!" Abbi groaned. "He knows how important this play is to me."

"He probably just went along for the fun of it," Blair said. "He seems to me a very shallow person."

"I always thought it was just an act," Abbi said.

"I guess I have a lot to learn about people."

Blair nodded sympathetically.

"I'll get Dan to help," Abbi said. "We'll find Matt after his dance rehearsal, and we'll go right up and ask him. Can you come, too?"

"Sorry," Blair said. "My lift will be waiting. But good luck!"

Dan was fixing a broken lace in his shoe when Abbi tracked him down at rehearsal. "What!" he exploded, when Abbi told him about her notebook. "You must be crazy! Matt wouldn't do a thing like that!"

"I didn't think so, either, but Blair–"

"Blair?" Dan raised his eyebrows. "What's she got to do with this?"

"She overheard Jenna and Lauren egging Matt on," Abbi said. "Dan, I've just got to find my book. I think Monsieur Le Blanc may have already called my mother."

Dan yanked his shoelace tight. "You're right. Finding the book is the first thing." He narrowed his eyes and squinted at Abbi. "After that, we need to get to the bottom of this."

"Thanks." Abbi squeezed his hand. "What would I do without friends like you, and Blair?" she added.

☆CHAPTER ELEVEN☆

Lost

Abbi and Dan ran down the hall towards Matt's locker.

"Matt," Abbi panted, "have you seen my French notebook?'

Matt was trying to pile too much into too small a space, and books and papers kept sliding off the shelf of his locker faster than he could push them back.

"No," he grunted. "Is it lost?"

"You know it is," Abbi accused, "because you took it, didn't you?"

Matt turned, in surprise, and let the contents of the top shelf slide to the floor behind him with a thud.

"*What*?" he said. "That French notebook you were so proud of yesterday? Why would I take it?"

"Forget why!" Abbi said. "Just tell me what you did with it."

"I thought you were handing it in," Matt looked puzzled.

"I did. But the classroom was empty and I left it on Monsieur Le Blanc's desk. And he says he never saw it. So somebody must have come in after I left, and taken it."

"And what makes you think this person was me?" Matt looked from Abbi to Dan.

"Blair Michaels said she heard you planning to take my book with Jenna and Lauren." Abbi stood in front of him with her hands on her hips, glaring.

"*Blair Michaels*," Matt breathed, nodding. "Well, that explains it."

"Explains what?"

"I thought you were smart, Abbi. Figure it out. In the meantime, would you like to go through my locker and look for your French book? Here, go through my bag, too." He tossed her his bag.

"You could have put it somewhere else..."

"Like the Lost and Found? Let's go and check." Matt turned and started down the corridor, walking with his fast dancer's stride. "I'm surprised at you, Dan, believing this story," he spat out over his shoulder.

"I didn't say I believed anything," Dan shrugged. "I just want to help Abbi get her book back. Otherwise, she's going to get kicked out of the show."

They had reached the bin on the second floor where the lost property was put. It was a tangle of forgotten junk.

Abbi dived in, throwing sweaters, scarves and gym shoes aside.

"Watch out!" Matt said cynically. "I hear there are cockroaches down there at the bottom."

Abbi stood up, her notebook clutched in one

hand, her face flushed. Furiously, she brushed off the cover.

"You knew exactly where to look, didn't you?" she accused him.

Matt looked stunned. "What – it was really there!"

"Of course it was. Right where you put it!" Abbi blazed. "I thought you were my friend, Matt." Abbi was turning the pages of her precious French book.

"I was." Matt's voice was husky with emotion. "But friends trust each other. You'd better think twice about who you trust these days!" Anger was very close to the surface of Matt's voice as he walked away. "You never know, we might actually have a blood-sucking vampire loose in the school."

Abbi stared after him. "Is he trying to say he still didn't take my book – even when he brought us right to it?" she asked Dan.

"Let's go and see if Monsieur Le Blanc is in his classroom," he said. "The sooner you hand that thing in, the better."

☆

Blair was late for rehearsal *again*, and this time, Mr Steel really was furious. Today, they were at last going to get all the dancers and singers on stage with the actors.

"Let's begin without her," Mr Steel stormed. "We have a lot to do. Abbi, can you stand in for Mina again?"

"OK," Abbi said. By now she knew all of Blair's blocking as well as her lines. "Can I make a suggestion?" Abbi took a deep breath. "Can Maeve do my part? When Mina and the maid are both on stage I get confused."

"Maeve, do you know the maid's blocking?" Mr Steel said gruffly.

Maeve came out of the prompter's box and stood on stage, her face flushed. "I think so," she said.

"Well, let's give it a try." Mr Steel paced up and down. "I hope you've all learned something from this experience. I hope you'll never forget that if one member of the cast or crew comes late, or doesn't show up, it can ruin a whole production!"

There was silence on the stage. Abbi felt tears prickling at the back of her eyes. She hadn't meant to start Mr Steel picking on Blair again. If she wasn't there she must have a good reason. Still, she had to admit it was true. It was hard to get the play going when people had to keep changing parts.

☆

Maeve was very good as the maid. She had re-membered all Abbi's gestures and looks in her funny scenes with Dan.

But Abbi hardly noticed. She was caught up in playing Mina to Jake's new, inspired Dracula. She could feel how much more relaxed Jake was when he didn't have to act with Blair.

When it was time for the dancers and chorus to come on, Abbi blinked as if she was waking from a powerful dream.

"Wish us luck," she heard Jenna whisper to Marcia. "We've been rehearsing in the dance studio, but Mr Steel hasn't seen our dances yet."

Abbi wanted to reach for Jenna's hand, to give it a reassuring squeeze, but there was this huge gulf between them. Jenna didn't even glance her way as the dancers swept on to the stage.

They were divided into two groups: Matt and his bats, wolves and spiders were the dark force, Jenna and her group represented the young people of the town. Each dance was like a duel, with the forces of good winning first, and then the forces of evil.

Jenna's group were all in red leotards, with silk banners that waved and flickered like flames. They forced back the creeping spiders, the snarling wolves and the dive-bombing bats. When the scene went black, the chorus of singers howled like defeated wolves.

Mr Steel stood up, applauding. "That's a fantastic effect!" he cried. "All right, singers, it's your turn – we might make a hit musical out of this yet!"

"Lauren has a solo," Dan whispered. "She wrote it herself."

Abbi gulped. She hadn't known anything about Lauren's song. How brave of Lauren, when she struggled with stage fright, Abbi thought. If I could just let her know I'm cheering for her; how I miss her, and Jenna!

All at once she missed the closeness with the others, with a sudden, awful pang. She found herself crossing her fingers for Lauren in the dark.

Lauren stood centre stage to sing. In the final production, there would be a white spotlight directly on her, and the rest of the chorus would fade into the background.

Abbi was crossing her fingers so tight they hurt. Lauren's song suited the play perfectly, but Abbi knew it was also about her problems with her parents.

When she had finished, Mr Steel applauded again. "That song gives me an idea," he said. "Why don't we have the dark dancers slowly surround you, as you sing. At the end, Matt will pick you up and carry you off to meet the beautiful lady in white who is the vampire. Let's try it."

"They make a lovely couple," Blair said, as they watched from the wings. She had arrived in the middle of the dance rehearsal.

Was Blair just being sarcastic? Abbi wondered. She hoped not. This was Lauren's dream come true – being swept up in Matt's arms. She found herself hoping that neither Blair or anyone else would spoil it for her.

"Abbi, you were wonderful as Mina tonight," Mr Steel said, when they had gathered on stage for the director's notes at the end of the rehearsal. "Because of you, we had a good – no, a great – rehearsal!" He turned to Blair. "And now I just have this to say. Anyone late or absent after this is out of the show for good!"

"I guess the great god Steel has spoken," Blair said, as he strode out of the theatre. She had a strange look in her eyes as she turned to Abbi. "Oh, by the way, thanks for standing in for me."

Abbi felt a lump in her throat. Just don't make

me do it again, she wanted to say.

She longed to hug Jenna and Lauren, to congratulate them on their parts in the musical. She watched the two of them leave the stage together – tall, graceful Jenna and Lauren, who seemed to be walking on air. How did I lose their friendship? she wondered miserably to herself.

☆

Lauren went home in a daze. She relived the moment over and over in her mind – first her song, floating over the auditorium, and then Matt's arm round her waist, scooping her up as if she weighed nothing.

"I've never heard you sing like that before!" he had whispered.

She hadn't ever sung like that, with her whole heart.

Lauren was in such a haze of happiness she hardly noticed the faces of her parents, as they waited for her inside the house.

She was on her way upstairs when her father said, "Lauren, we need to talk to you."

Not now! Lauren wanted to scream. Don't spoil this moment for me. But she could tell by her father's tone that it would be now.

"Lauren, Miss Bainbridge is talking about dropping you from her singing lessons," her father was saying.

"She says you haven't been practising!" Her mother hovered anxiously next to her father.

"Well, that would save you a lot of money," Lauren shrugged. She knew how much private singing lessons cost.

"Lauren! You know we don't care about the expense. We're talking about your whole life, here." Her father reached for her arm as she stood, poised on the second step of the staircase.

"No we're not!" Lauren shot back. "This whole opera thing was your idea. I've written my own song now. Not some dusty old thing, but a song about me. Maybe it's not Mozart, but I'm going to sing it."

Lauren ran up the rest of the stairs and slammed the door of her room. What would her parents think, if they knew that she would trade a lifetime of singing lessons for just one more chance to be close to Matt like she had been today.

☆

Dan and Abbi stood on the William S. Holly School steps, watching Blair's sports car pull away.

"That was a great rehearsal," Dan said. "I think the maid and gardener are really coming alive now. He loves you, but you reject him like some dirt beneath your feet. It's brilliant."

"You've made it come alive. They're all your ideas." Abbi sighed an enormous sigh. "Dan, I miss everybody. Jenna and Matt and Lauren. Seeing them all at rehearsal today reminded me."

"I miss them, too," Dan shrugged.

"I guess there's no chance we'll all get back together after *Dracula*?" Abbi went slowly down the steps. She watched the red car disappear round the corner. "Blair says I've just gone on to a higher plane of acting – and when you do that, you always leave people behind." She looked round at Dan. He had a very strange look on his face.

"Not you, Dan!" Abbi ran back up to him. "Nothing can split us up."

"And no one better try!" Dan said. "But I have the feeling they will." Abbi was already flying down the stairs again and didn't hear the rest of what Dan was saying. "I'm the last friend you've got but I can feel the grim hand of Blair Michaels tightening around my throat."

☆CHAPTER TWELVE☆

Disaster!

Abbi noticed Blair's empty chair in front of the lighted mirror in the dressing-room. Tonight, they were supposed to learn how to do their own make-up.

Where was she? If Mr Steel found out Blair was late...!

At that moment, Mrs Paynter, the make-up teacher, bustled in with a large metal box. When she opened it, she revealed layers of trays with tubes, jars and sticks of make-up, brushes, fake hair and glue.

"Every character in *Dracula* has special make-up," Mrs Paynter said briskly. "I'll just have time to show you once, so please remember to listen and make notes." She quickly laid out her supplies in a neat row.

Abbi crossed her fingers, hoping Blair would arrive before Mrs Paynter noticed she was missing.

"We'll begin with Dracula," she was saying.

Abbi breathed a sigh of relief. Blair had a few more minutes.

"We want Dracula to look pale and dangerous."

Mrs P whipped out a tube of make-up, squirted some on a sponge, and dabbed it across Jake's forehead.

Jake jerked back. "UGH! I hate this stuff!"

"Blend!" Mrs Paynter ordered, handing him the sponge. "Now we will transform you into an evil Count, hundreds of years old!"

The others watched in fascination as she sculpted hollows under Jake's cheekbones, made his nose long and his mouth scarlet. He twitched and squirmed when she drew on his eyelids, but when he opened his eyes they seemed to have sunk back in his head.

"You look terrible!" Abbi breathed.

Jake smiled and showed his fangs. The effect was truly terrifying.

"Good. It's all tricks of the light," Mrs Paynter stepped back from her work. "Who's next?"

She turned to Dan. "You're the gardener, right? What a wonderful face!" She held Dan's jaw firmly in her hand, studying him. "You'll grow into this face," she told him. "When all the other guys who think they're handsome now are podgy and boring, you'll be the one women will sigh for."

Abbi opened her eyes wide in surprise and stared at Dan's profile beside her. That nose? That mouth? Good-looking?

"Here," said Mrs Paynter, catching Abbi's expression, "I'll show you." She added some shadows and highlights to Dan's face. "Did you ever notice how the most adorable babies grow into the most ordinary-looking adults? That's

☆**84**☆

because we're not meant to look like babies all our lives. We need faces with some character."

"There! What do you think?" she stepped back from her work and looked at Dan's face in the mirror.

It was like looking at a computer image of Dan in the future. He looked…so strong. His eyes caught Abbi's, and something flashed between them that made her look away.

"But of course, for this play, you are just a humble gardener," Mrs Paynter said, picking up her sponge. "So, we'll scruff you up a bit." She finished with a flourish and stepped back, satisfied. "There," she smiled.

"Thanks," Dan grinned. "Poor and scruffy, that's me."

"Now!" Mrs Paynter turned to the empty chair. "Where is Blair Michaels, our star?"

There were murmurs and grumbles from the row of cast members in front of the row of lighted mirrors.

"Late, again…" Marcia said.

Blair! Come on! Abbi breathed, crossing her fingers once more.

"Well?" Mrs Paynter demanded. "Blair's make-up is tricky. So where is the girl?"

There was an awkward silence, then suddenly they heard Blair shouting at Geordie, the actor who played her fiancé.

"If you trip over my feet one more time, Geordie," Blair shouted, "I'm going to see to it personally that you never get a job in a professional theatre, oh!" She burst into the dressing-room and then stopped, realizing they had all heard her.

"We have just seen Blair Michaels transformed into a monster without the aid of make-up," Marcia said, acidly.

Blair glared at her and sat down.

"I h-h-hate her," Jake stammered as he and Dan left the dressing-room together. His stutter was back, Dan noticed, and it seemed to be worse.

"C-could you do s-s-something for m-me?" Jake asked, taking a pitifully long time to get the words out. He handed Dan some large empty capsules and a small bottle of red fluid.

"You want me to fill these capsules with stage blood for you?" Dan asked. "Sure. It must be hard to do anything with your hands with those fake fingernails glued on!"

Mrs Paynter had given Dracula long, evil-looking talons. They were glued securely to his own fingernails so they wouldn't come off on stage, but that meant Jake had to wear them from now to the end of the performance.

Jake grinned. "They g-get me out of a l-lot of w-w-ork!" he grinned. "Th-thanks."

Dan shoved the capsules into his pocket. He hoped Jake would get his confidence back during the dress rehearsal. Blair's effect on him was poison.

Abbi stayed with Blair in the dressing-room while she put the finishing touches to her make-up for Mina.

"That was a bore, almost being late again," Blair brushed off the awkward incident. "But wait till I tell you why I was late. I finally have some news about your audition..."

She lightly pencilled one eyebrow, sat back and checked the effect.

Abbi could hardly sit still. *What?* she wanted to shout.

"I was over at the studio," Blair went on, "and I overheard the producer say he definitely wants to find a replacement for – I still can't tell you her name," she smiled at Abbi in the mirror. "It would be unprofessional. Anyway, I gave him your picture, and he said he might call."

"When will I know?'

"They have to start shooting new episodes of *My Life* in January," Blair shrugged, "so it should be any day."

She applied white powder and turned to Abbi. "Be sure not to tell anyone," Blair warned. "I'd be in trouble if they found out I leaked the information."

"I won't," Abbi promised.

But she was bursting to tell Dan. *This* was why Blair was special, why they all had to make allowances for her being late...she was always doing something so important!

☆

Later, during rehearsal, Blair grabbed Dan's arm backstage. "I have to talk to you," she whispered.

"Sure," Dan whispered back. "I'll meet you downstairs at the break."

"No, that's no good. Abbi will be looking for me." Blair pulled him to one side. "The reason I was late was that I was out at the studio where they film *My Life*. I overheard someone say they need a guy for a small part – just two days shooting – so I suggested you!"

"Oh...?" said Dan. What was Blair up to now?

"Auditions are tomorrow morning. I think you'd have a great chance for this part. You're made for TV acting, Dan."

"Why don't you want Abbi to hear this?" Dan asked suspiciously.

"This is so embarrassing, but I've been promising to get Abbi an audition for *My Life*, and now it looks like it's fallen through. She's going to be crushed!" She passed Dan a business card. "The name of the producer is on here. Just tell him I sent you, and tell Abbi you heard about it through someone else."

Dan took the business card. "I don't like keeping secrets from my friends," he said.

"But you *have* to," Blair insisted. "Abbi will be so disappointed that she didn't get an audition and you did."

"Why did you get her all excited, if it wasn't a sure thing?"

"It was a sure thing, until I took in her picture..." Blair looked down at her feet.

"And...?" Dan asked.

"You're making this so hard. They said Abbi was too tall, too, too..."

"Big for the part?" Dan asked.

"Yes," Blair murmured. "Now do you see why you can't tell her?"

"I see..." Dan looked hard at Blair. "It was kind of you to take in Abbi's photo."

"I know how cruel they can be!" Blair said. "How they never think about how you feel – just too big, too small, wrong hair, too old..."

"Well, thanks for thinking of me," Dan tapped the business card. "But I don't think so. We have tech rehearsal tomorrow."

"That's too bad," Blair tipped her blonde head to one side. "They pay serious money for a part like that."

Dan's eyebrows shot up to his hair line. He thought about all the things that money like that would buy. "How could I get out there, audition and be back before rehearsal?"

"No problem." Blair said. "It's not far. The address is on the card."

"And you're sure about the money?"

"Of course!" Blair looked up at him. "There's major money to be made in TV."

Dan stared at her. He didn't trust Blair, but if there was even the slightest chance she was serious, he had to take it. He needed that money.

"OK," Dan swallowed hard. "Thanks."

"Then you'll go? That's great." Blair was beaming again. "You'll have time to get there and back before the tech rehearsal. Just be sure not to tell Abbi."

Dan hated to keep secrets, but Blair was right. As he watched Abbi come floating backstage, flushed and beaming from her scene, he knew he couldn't tell her. It would kill her to know what the producer had said about her. If nothing happened tomorrow, she'd never need to know. If it did, he'd find a way to explain.

Dan shook himself. What was happening to him? This is exactly how Blair wanted him to think – that this was his big break, and Abbi didn't matter.

"Big money!" Dan whispered to himself. It would mean they could pay the three months' back rent they owed. The landlord had been threatening to evict them. And maybe, there would be more work. Blair said he was made for TV acting – maybe it was true.

"Who am I kidding?" Dan groaned. "They'll probably just say 'too short, too skinny, and your ears stick out – get lost!'"

"But what should I do?" Dan murmured to himself. "I really need that money!"

☆CHAPTER THIRTEEN☆

Long Run

Dan stuffed his watch with the broken strap into his pocket and ran out of the door. An APARTMENT FOR RENT sign was staked to the lawn of the battered old house where he lived with his father. So it was true, the landlord *was* throwing them out at the end of the month!

He had to go to the TV audition. If he got this part today, he'd come home and pull up that sign himself!

Dan hopped on a bus at the corner of his street. It had been hard finding the fare to the audition and back, but he had just enough money.

My Life Productions was on the other side of the city. Dan took the bus to the train, then the train to the end of the line, and another bus to an old industrial area.

The TV production offices and studio were in a renovated factory with scrubbed brick walls.

Dan glanced at his watch. It had taken him over an hour to get there. That meant he must be back on the bus before twelve to make it to the tech rehearsal for *Dracula*.

Inside, an elegant metal staircase led up to a marble floor and a curved desk. On the walls hung photos of the leading *My Life* actors – including Blair, as Jackie.

A cool receptionist looked at the card, twitched a little when Dan mentioned Blair's name, and led him into a small waiting room with no windows.

"Have a seat," she said. "I'll tell Mr Mercantros you're here."

☆

Abbi slept late. She was woken by the sound of the door bell.

"It's somebody called Blair," Joe announced, thumping into her room. "She wants to come up." He bounced on Abbi's bed. "Mrs Thomas is already here," he moaned. "Can you tell her not to make me eat that porridge?"

Abbi didn't even hear him. Blair was at the door! She made a dive for the intercom, pressed the button, breathed "Blair, come on up", and raced back to her bedroom to throw on some clothes. She'd wear her best white shirt and new jeans...

Blair came waltzing through the door looking like someone in a TV Fashion Show.

"Wow!" said Joe, speechless for once.

"I thought we could go out for brunch before the tech rehearsal," Blair said. "If you have time."

Abbi had promised to clean her room, dust the living room and help Mrs Thomas look after Joe.

"Sure," she gasped. "I'm not doing anything." She blurted goodbye to Mrs Thomas and Joe, grabbed up her bag and followed Blair downstairs.

Incredibly, Blair had the red sports car. "This is my mum's friend, Dominique." She introduced Abbi to the man behind the wheel. "He drives for us sometimes."

Abbi felt as though she'd been whisked off to paradise. The feeling of being in heaven lasted through the drive to a restaurant in town, even though Blair sat in the front and she was doubled up in the tiny back seat.

There was expensive white linen on the restaurant tables and a red rose in each narrow vase. Abbi went back to the brunch buffet three times. There were hot fresh croissants and chocolate-coated strawberries.

"Sure you can't eat any more?" Blair asked.

"I'm absolutely stuffed," Abbi sighed blissfully. "Is this what it's like, being a TV star?"

"Well, I can't eat breakfast like this every day," Blair laughed. She'd only had a slice of melon and a glass of orange juice. "I'd soon weigh a ton!"

Abbi thought guiltily of the chocolate strawberries.

"Have you spoken to Dan this morning?" Blair asked, casually sniffing the rose.

"No," Abbi said. "Why?"

"I just wondered." Blair twirled the rose stem in her hand. "He told me he had something terribly important to do this morning, but he wouldn't tell me what. I thought he might have told you."

"No." Abbi shook her head. Dan usually told her everything.

"Well, never mind." Blair put the rose back in the vase. "I'm sure we'll find out. Do you want to go shopping? I have so much trouble finding things in my size," she sighed. "I have to go to the kids' section half the time."

"Shopping?" Abbi said. "I...I didn't bring any money."

"No credit cards?" said Blair as if the idea of going out without money was completely strange. "That's OK," she shrugged. "We don't have much time before the tech rehearsal anyway. Won't Mr Steel be surprised when I'm on time!"

☆

Dan pulled out his watch and stared at it. Eleven o'clock already. Time seemed to crawl by in the *My Life* company waiting room. If that audition didn't happen soon, he would have to leave! To come all this way for nothing...that couldn't happen.

Dan got up and paced the floor. Why didn't someone come? Finally, he pushed open the door and walked back down the carpeted hall to the receptionist's desk. No one was there.

Dan waited. He glanced at the desk quickly, to see if there was a message about his audition. A schedule – anything!

Blair's name at the top of a document caught his eye. It was some kind of memo – maybe this was it? Dan edged around the desk so he could read it.

Suddenly, he felt his feet freeze to the carpet as he read:

STRICTLY CONFIDENTIAL
Blair Michaels and her agent have been

*informed that her character in My Life
is being terminated. Jackie will die in a
boating accident...*

Dan's eyes skimmed over the rest of the details.
His eyes froze on one phrase: ***Miss Michaels' recent
mature look has forced this decision.***

Blair was losing her series because she looked
too old! She had no power to get him or anyone
else an audition. The producer had probably
forgotten he was even here. The whole thing had
been lies – a trick! But why?

Dan's eyes swept anxiously round the elegant
lobby. A large clock on the wall behind him caught
his eye. It had no numbers, just gold hands on a
black face.

Could it...? No, it wasn't possible. It looked as if
the clock said twelve-twenty. It must be wrong!

Dan pulled his watch out of his pocket. It still
said eleven o'clock. He shook it. The watch had
stopped. This clock was right! He'd be late for tech
rehearsal. Dan felt sickening waves of anger and
panic sweep over him. He had been set up by
Blair, just like the others.

The carpeted lobby was still completely
deserted. Dan glanced over to the desk and saw a
fax machine set to one side. In a moment of
decision, Dan thrust the memo into the fax and
pressed COPY.

Just then, the big doors on the other side of the
room opened. Dan could hear loud voices.

"Make sure you get through to New York this
morning, Miss Dickens. I'd like to get that deal
sewn up!"

The memo was humming through the machine. Dan stretched out a hand. Should he wait for the copy, or run? He listened, tense and alert.

"Yes, Mr Mercantros, I'll get right on to it."

Dan got ready to run.

"There's just one other thing..." The heavy wooden doors swung slightly shut. The conversation was muffled now.

The copy had started to slide out of the fax machine, and Dan's fingers itched. One more second, two...

His eyes were fixed on the door. Mr Mercantros's voice was raised. "Tell him I don't have time!'

Dan grabbed the copy and flung himself down the metal staircase and out into the street without looking back. If the receptionist saw the original memo in the fax machine she might put two and two together and come after him.

He pounded down the block to the bus stop – but there was no bus in sight on the cold, windy street. Even if a bus came right now – he'd never make it back to William S. Holly in time.

☆

"I wonder why Dan isn't here?" said Abbi. "It's already twelve-thirty."

She had looked backstage, in the dressing-rooms, even up in the lighting booth – but no Dan. The tech crew were busy with the lighting, and the comfortable, familiar *Dracula* set seemed suddenly overrun with people and confusion.

"Dan's always early," Abbi told Blair. "I think I'll call him."

She came running back from the pay phone a few minutes later, a look of alarm on her face. "His telephone's been disconnected!" she gasped. "I wonder what's going on?"

Blair looked puzzled. "That's strange," she said. "Maybe you made a mistake."

"No, I tried three times," Abbi said. "Look, it's twelve-forty. I'm going to Dan's – he only lives a few streets away. I know he wouldn't be late unless something had happened to him."

Blair shook her head despairingly. "Oh, Abbi, I'm afraid you have too much faith in people."

"What do you mean?" Abbi demanded. "Dan would never let me down. He's my best–" She stopped and flushed red. "I'll be right back."

Abbi grabbed her jacket and raced up the slanted floor of the auditorium and out of the school. It had frozen overnight, and there were patches of ice on the pavement. What if Dan had been hurrying, too, and had slipped? Maybe he was hurt!

It was a quarter of a mile to Dan's house, but if she ran the whole way, she might just get there and back before the tech rehearsal started.

☆

Dan's bus growled slowly into the bus station. The clock there said twelve forty-five. There was no way he could make it to school on time.

Desperately, Dan fumbled through his pockets. If only he had some more change, he could call the school and let them know. But it had taken all his money just to pay the bus fare.

There was nothing in his pockets now but the stupid stage blood capsules he had filled for Jake. On top of everything else, if he didn't make it to rehearsal, Jake wouldn't have his fake blood when he bit Blair!

Dan looked hopelessly around the busy station. If only the stupid clock would just stop ticking! He pictured Mr Steel, stony-faced, as he tried to explain. And Abbi! She would find out where he had gone. She would never forgive him!

He had to do *something*. He couldn't just stand here and let Blair win!

☆CHAPTER FOURTEEN☆

Desperate Tactics

Abbi skidded to a stop on the icy pavement. This couldn't be Dan's house – shabby, run down, with an APARTMENT FOR RENT sign on it.

Abbi was breathing hard after her long run. 67 Lombard Street – she'd seen the address on all Dan's notebooks. This *must* be it.

She marched up the rickety stairs and looked at the names over the doorbells. There were three cards under the bells. The top one said REEVE in Dan's neat writing.

Abbi took a deep breath and pushed the buzzer. There was no answer. She pushed it again, and again. Someone must answer, she whispered to herself.

Someone must explain why there was a FOR RENT sign on Dan's house. Why his phone was cut off, why Dan wasn't at the rehearsal! It was as if he'd totally disappeared.

She had to find him, and time was running out. If he wasn't at rehearsal in a few minutes, he'd be out of the show. And so would she!

☆

Dan stood helpless on the station platform, staring at the clock. "You're an actor," a small voice whispered inside his frantic brain. "So ACT!"

Dan whipped the fake blood capsules out of his pocket. He put one in his mouth and bit down, hard.

Red goo spurted out of his mouth, down his chin and over his jacket. It had no taste at all, Dan noticed.

"Help!" Dan gave a choking, but very loud shout, and slumped forward. He was careful to fall just the way they'd been trained in movement classes. It looked dramatic, but he landed unhurt.

Dan put two more capsules in his mouth and bit again. More fake blood. A lot of blood this time.

Almost immediately, a crowd gathered round him. "Somebody get an ambulance!" cried a woman.

Then things started to happen very fast.

Nobody talked to Dan, or tried to ask him questions. Within minutes, he found himself wrapped in a blanket on a stretcher in the back of a speeding ambulance, with a blue-jacketed ambulance attendant about to plunge a needle into his arm.

"Wait!" Dan spat out the capsules, and tried unsuccessfully to sit up. "No needles! I'm OK, really I am!"

"What?" The attendant's face changed from relief to surprise.

Dan held out the last full capsule from his pocket. "It's just stage blood," he said. "I'm fine, but it *is* a matter of life and death. I need a fast ride to the William S. Holly Stage School."

The attendant leaned forward and spoke through a sliding panel to the driver. Then he turned and looked stonily at Dan.

"Start talking, kid!" he said. "And this had better be good!"

☆

The door swung inwards so hard that Abbi almost fell into the dim hall.

"What do you want?" growled a voice.

"Hi, I'm Dan's friend, Abbi," she stammered. Could this be Dan's father? He had grey hair and there was stubble on his chin. He looked as if he'd been sleeping in his clothes.

"Dan's not here," the man said. "He went racing off to some darn fool audition on the other side of town. Dreaming of big money. I told him it was a waste of bus fare, but oh no, he had to go."

"An...audition?" Abbi said. "Are you sure it wasn't a rehearsal?"

"Nah! He says he's going on TV now, going to make lots of money. I got to shut this door. It's cold out there."

The door slammed in Abbi's face. She turned and ran, down the steps and along the slippery pavement, back towards Stage School. Dan at an audition! What did it mean?

☆

"I suppose what it means," said Blair, "is that he really doesn't care about our show."

"His father said he went to an audition! I just

can't believe it." Abbi paced the dressing-room floor, her face still red from her mad dash through town.

"You'd better get your make-up on," Marcia stuck her head round the door and shouted. "Mr Steel says he wants to check us all under the lights."

"But where was the audition?" Abbi muttered to herself. "And how did Dan know about it?" She sat down in front of the make-up mirror, her head in her hands.

"She told me," said a voice from the doorway behind her. Abbi looked up, startled.

A figure appeared suddenly beside her in the mirror. A figure with his face and jacket streaked with blood, his hair standing on end, and his eyes burning with anger. One skinny finger was pointing straight at Blair.

"She did!" the figure croaked again, and then collapsed into a chair.

"DAN!" shrieked Abbi. "What happened? You're hurt!"

"Don't worry, it's fake blood, just like the audition was fake. Blair sent me out to the *My Life* studios for an audition that never happened, but would have made me just late enough to get kicked out of **Dracula**."

Abbi stared at both of them. "You sent Dan on a *My Life* audition and didn't tell me?" she shouted at Blair. "And you *went* to an audition and didn't tell me?" she accused Dan. "I've been running round in the cold because I thought something terrible had happened to you. I thought you were my friends!"

Blair tossed her head. Her eyes narrowed. "Don't get so excited," she said. "The director looked at your picture and said you seemed too mature for the part."

"You mean too big!" Abbi cried. She stared at Dan and Blair. "He said I was too fat for TV!"

"Don't believe her," Dan said. "She probably didn't even show your picture to the director. They want a little kid for that part – someone who looks really young–"

"Stop!" Abbi screeched at him. "I don't want to talk to you. I can't believe you did this to me!"

☆CHAPTER FIFTEEN☆

Battle Plan

"I nearly killed myself trying to find you," Abbi dashed the tears out of her eyes. "Blair was right. I trust people too easily."

"Abbi, I'm sorry!" Dan shouted, as she pushed her way past them to join the others on stage.

"What's the matter with your make-up, Abbi?" Mr Steel thundered at her when she stood under the stage lights. "You're as red as a brick. Go back and tone it down."

Abbi stumbled off stage. She hadn't had a chance to put on any make-up. The red was pure rage and embarrassment and the result of running for ten minutes.

"I have no friends now," she gulped to herself, slapping white powder on her flushed cheeks. "What a stupid idiot I've been!"

It was almost as if the tech rehearsal was a mirror of her wild emotions. Nothing worked; the lighting panel blew up, plunging the whole theatre into darkness. Then the fog machine went crazy and thick grey fog covered everything in sight.

Geordie tripped over Blair again, and Blair

stormed off the stage. Finally, Jake's one remaining capsule burst too soon, dribbling red goo down the front of Blair's costume.

"Where are the other capsules?" Mr Steel roared. "We're going to practise this bite until we get it right!"

It took hours to get it right. Dan had to make more capsules, and Jake's stutter got worse by the minute. The other actors sat glumly backstage with the dancers and chorus while Blair and Jake went over and over the fatal vampire bite.

Abbi stood by herself, not looking at the others.

"What's wrong with her?" Marcia whispered to Dan.

Dan glanced at Abbi. She looked so different from her normal lively self that he felt sick. "She just lost her best friend," Dan murmured.

"Blair? It's about time!" Marcia said with feeling.

Abbi gave Dan a bitter look as they filed on stage for Mr Steel's final notes on the rehearsal. Dan seemed to have found another friend fast! thought Abbi.

"That was the worst technical rehearsal I have ever seen," Mr Steel told them. "I want you to go home now, rest tomorrow, and come back for Monday night's dress rehearsal determined not to let any of this happen again."

The performers drifted off stage, their shoulders slumped and heads hanging down.

"Matt, wait!" Dan ran up behind him. "I want to call a meeting, at your place, tomorrow."

"What?" Matt turned. "You mean about *Dracula*?

We were terrible, weren't we?"

"No, it's about Blair Michaels," Dan explained. "Can we meet in your basement? Jenna, Lauren, you and me?"

"Sure," Matt nodded. "It'll be like old times, except for–"

"Except for Abbi," Dan nodded, grimly. "She's the reason I want to get together. "

☆

Sunday morning, Matt showed them into his basement den, decorated with posters of rock musicians and filled with comfortable old furniture. "OK, Dan," he said, "what's this all about?"

"*Dracula* is a mess," Dan said. "None of us are friends with Abbi any more and we're hardly friends with each other. Did any of you ever wonder what happened?"

Jenna tossed back her black braids. "Abbi's been a pain since she started hanging around with Blair."

Lauren said nothing. She didn't want to talk about her battle with Abbi, especially in front of Matt.

"She accused me of taking her French book," Matt shrugged. "How could she think I'd do a thing like that?"

"Blair made her think it," said Dan. "And Blair made Jenna think she was dieting, and Lauren think – " he caught Lauren's pleading glance. "Well, never mind the details. I think Blair was behind all our fights with Abbi. I got sucked into one of her schemes yesterday, so I know how it feels."

He quickly filled them in on the details of his trip to the *My Life* studios and back. "They nearly threw me out of the ambulance when they found out it was fake blood," he said. "But then they got another call near the school and I convinced them to drop me off. I've never done such a good acting job in my life, but all it accomplished was keeping me in the show. Abbi's still convinced I let her down. She won't even speak to me."

"I think you're right," Jenna's eyes were fiery. "Blair separated us from Abbi, one by one. Marcia warned me she might try something like this. She likes to find someone she can completely dominate, someone who will worship her. Then, if they get too good, she turns on them."

"That's exactly what's happening with Abbi," Dan nodded.

"How can we stop her?" Matt said.

"We can confront her, tomorrow night at dress rehearsal," Dan suggested. "If you're all with me."

"What if she just laughs at us?" said Lauren.

"I don't think she will." Dan patted his pocket. "I have a secret weapon."

☆

The cast of *Dracula* was getting ready for dress rehearsal. This was their last chance, Abbi thought, to get it right. Tomorrow was the opening night!

"Honestly, Abbi, I didn't know Dan was going to audition," Blair said. "I happened to mention they were looking for a male actor, that's all. Dan must have called the studio. But I could have told him it was crazy to try to get there before the tech rehearsal."

Abbi had promised herself she wouldn't listen to any apologies, but she couldn't resist Blair's wide-eyed, innocent look. Maybe, after all, Blair was a true friend.

☆

"I don't think you quite understand." Jenna stood with her hands on her hips in front of Blair. "We want you to tell Abbi that you threw her French notebook in the lost property bin, and that you sent Dan halfway across the city on a fake audition, on purpose." Jenna leaned towards her.

"I don't know what you're talking about!" Blair backed up against the make-up counter. "I'm not telling Abbi anything!"

"Then maybe you won't mind if I show her this...?" Dan held up his copy of the confidential memo.

"Where...where did you get that?" Blair's face turned white. "Give it to me!"

"No," said Dan. "But I'm going to give it to Abbi. She's going to know there was never a chance that she'd get a part on *My Life*. They want someone who looks like a little girl to replace you."

Blair's face twisted. "You're all so infantile. Tell Abbi whatever you like. She's starting to bore me, anyway."

"Tomorrow," Dan said menacingly, "is opening night. We want *you* to tell her before the show! Otherwise – this goes public!"

☆CHAPTER SIXTEEN☆

The Big Night

Mr Steel had asked the whole cast to come early to the theatre on opening night.

"There are people out there!" Maeve's terrified face appeared in the make-up room mirrors. "The whole auditorium is filling up!"

A tremor of fear ran around the make-up room. Abbi felt her eyeliner pencil jump, and one eyebrow shot up her forehead. It felt so strange not to have Dan at her elbow, teasing and making jokes. He'd done his make-up early and gone backstage.

At that moment, Jake came through the dressing-room doors, his long black cape streaming out behind him. "Has anybody s-seen Blair?" he asked. "I want to go over that scene where I have the blood capsules in my mouth, just before I b-bite her. It's hard to talk with them in my mouth with these t-teeth."

A silence fell over the dressing-room.

"Blair isn't here yet," said Jenna, finally. "We'll let her know you're looking for her, Jake."

Just then, Mr Steel came through the door.

"I've come to tell everybody to break a leg," he said. "I also wanted you to know the fog machine and lights are working brilliantly tonight, so things should go smoothly–" He stopped suddenly and looked around the dressing-room. "Where is Miss Michaels?"

Something in his voice made them freeze and glance guiltily at each other.

"It's twenty to eight," Mr Steel said. "Where is Blair Michaels? Has anyone seen her tonight?"

Nobody wanted to say what was obvious. No one *had* seen her. Blair was late.

Abbi gripped her chair, expecting another explosion.

Instead, Mr Steel's voice was calm and level. "Right. Abbi, take your hair down. Change your make-up – a little paler, please, and get into Mina's costume for the first act. If Blair isn't here in five minutes, you're going on in her place."

"Mr Steel?" Abbi gaped at him. "Do you mean, take Blair's *place*, as Mina? I can't–"

"Of course you can. Luckily, her first act costume is a dressing gown – it should fit you OK. By the second act, we'll have Mina's other costume adjusted to fit you."

"But..." Abbi stammered.

"I told Blair to be here at seven like the rest of you, and she's not here. If she isn't here by seven forty-five she's not going on at all!"

"But…what about the maid's part?" Abbi looked down at her costume – a black dress and neat white apron.

"Maeve, you can do the maid's part," Mr Steel said firmly. "And I'll take your place in the prompter's box."

The look of delight on Maeve's face frightened Abbi. This couldn't really be happening. She stood up, her legs shaking. "Mr Steel – everyone out there is expecting to see Blair Michaels. She's a big star..."

"Maybe that's the problem," he said. "Maybe they should be expecting to watch a play, not a star. My decision is final." He looked round at the stunned faces. "I expect the rest of you to work together and help Abbi and Maeve every way you can. Curtain in twenty minutes." And he whirled away, banging the door behind him.

Jenna, Lauren and Matt stared at each other. This was all their doing – theirs and Dan's. Blair was obviously late so she wouldn't have to make her speech to Abbi.

"Come on, Abbi," Marcia said. "You've stood in for Blair so many times you know her part better than she does." She led Abbi to the girls' dressing-room, where all the costumes were kept.

"I can't do it!" Abbi groaned, as hands reached out to loosen her hair and help her out of her maid's clothes.

"Are you ready?" Mr Steel stuck his head round the door again.

Abbi gulped. Did she really know Blair's lines, and her blocking? Mina was on stage for most of the play. Could she do it? Oh, Blair, Abbi begged inwardly. Don't let this happen. Please don't ruin our play. Please, *please* get here on time.

It took Abbi two long minutes to squirm into Blair's costume, pat powder on her cheeks, and run up the backstage stairs to wait in the wings. Everything was dark except for the stage manager's light in one corner. Now, the buzz of happy, excited conversation from the auditorium drowned out the pounding of her heart.

Mr Steel was there beside her, glancing at his watch. The seconds were ticking by. Seven forty-three, seven forty-four.

Mina's opening lines were racing through Abbi's brain:

> *Lucy, Lucy, where are you? What are those strange noises in the garden? The door is open... have you gone walking in your sleep again? Oh, Lucy, I'm so afraid for you... there's a cold mist out there.*

Abbi felt Mina's fear all mixed up with her own. Where was Blair? What had happened? Why wasn't she here?

"OK, that's it," Mr Steel said coldly. "Seven forty-five. Abbi, you're going on as Mina."

At that very moment, they heard light steps running up the stairs and into the darkness back stage. "Where's my costume?" It was Blair. "Abbi! They said you were up here. What are you doing in my costume?" she hissed.

"You're too late, Blair," Mr Steel said, stepping forward. "I warned you what would happen if you were late. Abbi's going on in your place tonight."

Blair was speechless. In the dim light, Abbi could

see her small face twisted with anger. "You can't..." she began.

"Yes I can. I'm the director."

"Blair, I'm *sorry*!" Abbi whispered desperately.

"Yes, Abbi's sorry and so am I, and so is the whole cast," said Mr Steel. "We're sorry you have so little regard for this production that you even show up late on opening night."

"If *she* goes on," Blair pointed at Abbi, "then I'm out of here, and I'm not coming back. She can have my part. It's what she's always wanted, anyway. After all I've done for you, this is how you pay me back!" She flung the words in Abbi's face, turned and stalked off down the stairs.

"Mr Steel?" Abbi said, trying not to burst into tears.

Even Mr Steel looked shaken. He stared after Blair.

"She's walking out on the whole play, you can't let her do that!" Abbi clutched his arm.

The buzz of expectant chatter from the other side of the curtain was growing louder. Mr Steel pulled it back for a peek.

"There's not an empty seat in the place." He took a deep breath. "They're looking forward to a good show and we're going to give them a good show. It's up to you now, Abbi."

The singers were filing past to take their position on stage. Lauren squeezed Abbi's hand as she went by. "You can do it," she whispered to her. Abbi gasped. It was the first time Lauren had spoken to her in weeks.

"I've got to get over to the prompter's box now," Mr Steel said. "When the chorus start the wolf howls, you cross to centre stage and get into bed. When the curtain goes up, you sit up and light the candle and deliver your opening lines. Got that?"

Abbi knew it, like she knew the whole play – inside out and back to front. If only she could get rid of this feeling of numb terror. Her tongue felt frozen to the roof of her mouth and her knees were shaking.

Another hand reached for hers in the darkness. Abbi felt Jake's long fingernails press into her palm. "I'm really glad it's going to be you," Jake bent down to whisper in her ear. There was no trace of his nervous stutter. "I think you're a much better Mina than she is..." The stage manager's light glinted on Dracula's fangs, and then Jake was gone.

In the darkness, Abbi could feel everyone in position, waiting. The backstage crew were at their posts, ready to hand props to the actors, ready with costume changes, ready with the flapping bats and the fog machine.

Jenna, Matt and the other dancers were in the wings on the other side of the stage. Their first dance was in a few moments, when Dracula attacked Lucy in the graveyard.

The house lights dimmed, and the stage went black. There were rustles and gasps from the audience as a huge, illuminated bat swooped from the balcony out over the audience. The chorus began their low chant, punctuated by wolf howls.

Abbi took a deep breath and felt her way across the stage and into the bed. As the wolf howls reached their high point, the curtain opened, and the lights came up slowly.

Abbi reached for the candle with trembling fingers. She would drop the match, it would go out. Then, somewhere inside her head, she heard Miss Madden, the acting teacher's voice say: *Use your fear, bring it into your performance...*

The candle sputtered, but lit. Abbi let the fear rush into her voice:

Lucy...Lucy, where are you?

Mina's desperate call rang out over the hushed theatre. The wolves howled again, and a pale green light lit the fog that came creeping into Mina's bedroom.

Dracula had started.

☆CHAPTER SEVENTEEN☆

Spotlight on Abbi

In the interval after the first act, the rest of the cast surrounded her.

"Abbi, Abbi, you were great!"

"Maeve, you were a fantastic maid!"

"We knew you could do it!"

Mr Steel still looked worried, but his voice was calm and reassuring. "It was a bit slow at the beginning, but that's normal for opening night. Actors, just pick up your cues a little faster in the second act. Everyone's doing well – the chorus is great, and dancers, you were very effective."

Abbi felt breathless, as though she had been running. Now that she'd started, she couldn't wait for the second act to begin. The costume crew had been working frantically sewing another panel on the bottom of Mina's skirt and letting out the jacket. She could just squeeze into it now.

"Mr Steel?" she asked. "Do I...do I look too big?"

"Whatever gave you that idea?" Mr Steel looked surprised. "You look fine. And on stage you project something electrifying across the footlights. It isn't something we can teach you here at Holly, it's something you're born with, Abbi."

"But, you said at auditions, that I was too big to play Lucy," Abbi insisted. She had to get this straightened out.

"I did? Yes, I guess I did. I meant that if Blair played Mina, you would overpower her. She would look like your little sister on stage. It was just the contrast between your heights."

Mr Steel looked very seriously into Abbi's eyes. "One thing you'll have to get used to in the theatre is the thoughtless, insensitive things directors say."

"That's OK," Abbi laughed, relief flooding through her. Mr Steel really was wonderful!

"Don't laugh!" the costume assistant cried. "I'm sewing you into this, and I want the stitches to hold."

"Stand by with the needle and thread!" Abbi sucked in her breath. "I may need repairs."

When the curtain rose again, Abbi was ready. The other actors had also got over their first night jitters. The act flew along, faster and better than it had ever done in rehearsals. Jake was a towering, menacing Dracula. Abbi had never had a feeling like this. By the time he swept her into his arms at the end of the second act, she could have floated right up through the ceiling.

☆

The curtain came down on the third act to thunderous applause. On stage, the actors gathered round Abbi, congratulating her.

"Wait!" Mr Steel called. "Curtain calls. Get into position."

They snapped back into the positions they had rehearsed, with Abbi and Jake in the centre, and the rest lined up on both sides. The curtain swept open and the audience rose to its feet. They cheered as the dancers took a bow, and then again for the singers.

The curtain calls went on and on. Abbi could feel bubbles of happiness burst inside her. So this is what it was all about, she thought. This feeling of joy so intense you thought you were going to fly. They had done it! And they would get to do it five more times.

When the last curtain call was over, the whole cast thundered down to the dressing-room, whooping and cheering and yelling like a winning football team. Matt leaped into the air and clicked his heels together.

"Save some of this for tomorrow night," Mr Steel tried to bellow over the noise. "You have five more performances to do!"

If it was five hundred, she'd be happy, Abbi thought. And if it was five thousand, she would never forget this first one. If only she could share it with her friends.

☆

The next morning, Abbi walked into the canteen as usual, looked across the room and stopped dead.

All her old group was sitting at their usual table.

"Abbi!" Jenna shouted. "Over here!"

"We have something to tell you," Lauren said as

Abbi approached. She was sitting beside Matt. "It's our fault Blair's out of the show. We teamed up against her." Lauren looked pleased.

"We made her confess that she'd broken up our friendship with you on purpose," Jenna added. "But I guess she didn't manage after all."

Abbi looked at her friends. They were all smiling, as if they'd done something marvellous. "I don't understand..." she began.

"Read this." Dan handed her a folded piece of paper. "Blair kept promising to get you an audition to replace a girl who was leaving *My Life*, right?"

"Right," Abbi said, reaching for the memo.

"I feel sorry for Blair," Lauren said. "But she let down the whole show, and she told lies to make you hate us. We couldn't let her get away with it, Abbi."

"She's been acting like a spoiled five-year-old," Matt added indignantly

Abbi finished reading the piece of paper. "I just can't believe it!" she gasped. "*Blair* was the girl! Blair looks too old...so they're going to axe her character." She slumped down at the table. "It's so cruel," she breathed.

"It is cruel," Dan agreed. "I discovered that waiting in the *My Life* studios. Imagine being rejected as an actor, just because you're growing up! Maybe that's why we all need Stage School – to give us time to grow before we have to handle all this stuff."

"There's nothing you can do about Blair being out of the show now." Jenna put her arm round

Abbi's shoulder. "But stop feeling guilty. It wasn't *your* fault."

"But it was!" Abbi groaned. "I was so impressed by Blair's fame and glamour and money. I was dazzled. Now I know where the expression *blind ambition* comes from!"

"You weren't the only one who was blinded by Blair," said Dan. "When she promised me mega bucks, I was over there like a shot."

"It's a good thing we don't need to earn money right now," Jenna said. "So we can all concentrate on learning, until we're older."

Abbi glanced at Dan. She wouldn't tell the others about his house, or his father or the FOR RENT sign. But she knew that money meant a lot to Dan right now.

"I'm sorry we're not as exciting as TV stars," Lauren said.

Abbi laughed shakily. "I thought being a TV star was so important. Now I know the most important thing is right here..." She looked round at them. " ...I've got my friends back."

Just then, Marcia came tearing across the canteen towards them. "Have you heard the news?" she said. "Blair Michaels is dropping out of school."

"Oh, no!" Abbi said. "Is it because of *Dracula*?"

"Probably," Marcia nodded. "She must be furious that you went on as the star of the show instead of her. Especially when you were so brilliant. Don't forget, she was a star when she was a little kid, so people treated her as if she was something really special. But then she started getting older – and other people were just as good."

"She saw Abbi as a threat?" asked Lauren.

"Maybe not at first. She's totally insecure, so she always has to have someone around who idolizes her. In this case it was Abbi. But then she saw Abbi had too much talent, so she had to find a way to put her down. The TV audition was perfect. She already knew herself how bad it felt to be rejected, just because you looked too old for a part."

Abbi's eyes misted over. "Blair knew how much that would hurt," she said, "because it had just happened to her." Abbi brushed her hand across her eyes. "I'm going to get a drink…anyone want something?"

Her friends shook their heads sympathetically as she walked away.

"I heard Blair was leaving," said Jenna. "I also heard she might be in a play in New York…"

"Or she might get a new TV series," added Matt. "In any case, she's outgrown her welcome at William S. Holly."

☆CHAPTER EIGHTEEN☆

Curtain Down!

It was closing night and Jenna was brushing Abbi's mass of gold-blonde hair. "Abbi?" she said, "I'm sorry we had that stupid fight about food. Blair just made me so mad – sometimes I think maybe I'm a bit like her. I want to be a famous dancer so badly."

"You're nothing like her!" Abbi's eyes flashed. "I'm so glad we're friends again. Are your mum and sister here tonight?"

Jenna nodded. "They're finally getting used to the idea of me being a dancer. And I'm finally getting used to the idea of being the world's tallest ballerina. What about your parents, Lauren?"

Lauren was at the other end of the make-up counter, studying her pale face. She nodded. "Even my brother Robert is out there," she said. "I really wish they hadn't come."

"Why? Don't you want to show off your song? It's great!" Jenna added a stroke of blusher to her high cheekbones.

"They won't think so," Lauren said. "But I don't care any more."

"That's the right attitude!" Matt put his arm round Lauren's shoulder. "You know you're good, that's what matters."

Lauren smiled up at him. It was amazing how just being near Matt had the power to make her dizzy with happiness.

"Well, my little brother will be in the front row," Abbi laughed. "And guess what? My French teacher, Monsieur Le Blanc, is coming. He told me I actually got an 'A' grade and he just had to come and see what inspired me."

There was a knock on the dressing-room door. It was Abbi's little brother, Joe, with an armful of red roses. "They're for you," he said, his eyes searching the room for Dracula. "Mum said I could bring them down."

"Come on in," Abbi laughed. "I know you want to meet Dracula. Jake, this is my little brother, Joe."

Joe reached out in awe to shake Jake's hand. Jake bowed formally. "Delighted to make your acquaintance," he said in his best Transylvanian accent.

Abbi was tearing open the card that had come with the roses. *Congratulations on your first part, kid,* it read. *Your Dad, from Down Under.*

Abbi buried her face in the roses, smelling their heady perfume. Her dad didn't even know she was the star of the show. It didn't matter. Whether she was the maid or the female lead, she was part of the performance with all the others. That's what counted!

"If only this could go on forever," she murmured.

"Well it might..." Dan pulled a cutting out of his pocket. "Did you see this? There's a city drama festival two months from now. We're just a junior school, but maybe we can talk Mr Steel into entering *Dracula: The Musical*."

Abbi jumped up. "Let me see that! Two more months of doing *Dracula*? We have to talk him into it." She waved the cutting at the others. "Any ideas? This could be our next Stage School triumph!"

Preview the next

STAGE SCHOOL ★

NOW...

Jenna – Dancing Dreams

☆CHAPTER ONE☆

Dance Partners

Jenna waited for her turn to go spinning across the long, bare dance studio floor. Every muscle was ready. Every bit of her body was tuned to the music of the grand piano at one end of the studio.

Suddenly a burst of laughter echoed around the large empty room. The piano music crashed to a halt.

"Matt!" called Ms Adaman, the dance teacher. "Save your socializing for later!"

Jenna's concentration was shattered. She glared across the room at tall, dark-haired Matt Caruso. As usual, he was surrounded by a group of giggling girls, the centre of attention, loving every minute of it.

"Is it my turn?" Matt called. "You want me to show the rest of them how it's done?"

I could strangle him, Jenna thought furiously. He's so conceited! It's not his turn.

But Matt had already launched into his spin, the music soared from the piano again, and Jenna caught her breath.

There was something so light and magic in Matt's dancing that he took your heart with him on his wild whirl across the wooden floor.

He came to rest staring straight into Jenna's eyes. He was the only student in the class, boy or girl, who was her own height.

"Well?" he asked.

"Your spin was all wrong..." Jenna said. "Your arms were in the wrong position, your torso wobbled, and your feet...!" Matt made her feel prickly, off balance. She wanted to wipe that smug grin off his face!

"All right, Jenna, it's your turn," Ms Adaman called.

Jenna took another deep breath. How could she concentrate now?

"Watch those arms," Matt teased. "Keep your spine straight!"

Jenna struggled to find her balance as the music began. She found herself gritting her teeth as she spun across the floor. She wanted so badly to do it right.

"That was technically perfect," Ms Adaman told her when she reached the other side of the room.

None of the others, especially Matt, understand what dancing means to Jenna. Where will her quest for dancing perfection take her? Read on in...

Stage School 3
☆Jenna – Dancing Dreams☆

Have you read the other Stage School stories?